KING OF THE MOLE PEOPLE

RISE OF THE SLUGS

KING OF THE MOLE PEOPLE

RISE OF THE SLUGS

BOOK 2

PAUL GILLIGAN

Christy Ottaviano Books

HENRY HOLT AND COMPANY

NEW YORK

To my favorite Up-worlders,
Eleni, Evan, and Rosa

Henry Holt and Company, *Publishers since 1866*
Henry Holt® is a registered trademark of Macmillan Publishing Group, LLC
120 Broadway, New York, NY 10271
mackids.com

Library of Congress Cataloging-in-Publication Data is available.

ISBN 978-1-250-17136-8

Our books may be purchased in bulk for promotional, educational, or business
use. Please contact your local bookseller or the Macmillan Corporate and
Premium Sales Department at (800) 221-7945 ext. 5442 or by email at
MacmillanSpecialMarkets@macmillan.com.

First edition, 2020
Designed by Cindy De la Cruz

Printed in the United States of America by LSC Communications,
Harrisonburg, Virginia

10 9 8 7 6 5 4 3 2 1

CONTENTS

KING OF THE
MOLE PEOPLE

RISE
OF THE
SLUGS

PROLOGUE

I kept telling them I didn't want to be King. I tried everything I could to get out of it. I tried pretending to be allergic to mud. I tried disguising myself with a wig and fake mustache. I tried telling them I'd been hit on the head and no longer knew how to speak English.

I told them I wasn't cut out to be King, and that the longer they made me do it, the greater the guarantee that something bad was going to happen.

But they just laughed. And I threw down my fake mustache and told them I didn't know what they thought was so funny.

Then I started thinking maybe they were

right. Maybe being King wasn't going to lead to disaster. Maybe my fear of bad things happening was all in my head.

And the next thing I knew I was staring at a collection of my friends engulfed in a huge, quivering slime globule.

I wanted to say "I told you so," but I doubted they could hear me.

1

MONDAY MORNING

I knew instinctively that time was up when a dead bird fell out of the sky. I don't know much about omens, but I do know weirdness pretty thoroughly, and that was completely weird.

It had been about three weeks since the world almost ended. Three weeks of me trying to get everyone to understand a couple of simple things:

1) I was a weirdness magnet.

And 2) Weirdness attracts more weirdness. You make a little room for things like talking to tombstones or eating eel burritos for lunch, and the next thing you know giant worms are

erupting beneath your feet and ripping everything to pieces.

For me, being King of the Mole People was
like being a walking time bomb.

I'd been trying to hand back the Mole crown
pretty incessantly. But the Moles said they
couldn't accept it back without another suitable
candidate. I pointed out that my humanness
rendered any of them a more suitable candidate
than me, and that I was giving them one month

to find somebody. They agreed, but I was suspicious. I'd seen a Mole calendar. It was just a rock with another rock on top of it.

OCTOBER SOMETHING

I realize I shouldn't have permitted it go on as long as I did, and that every day that went by increased the chances that the circling weirdness would become a vortex and destroy us all. But I'd developed a bit of a soft spot for the Moles, and like I said, I'd started deluding myself that maybe the danger was all in my head.

And then the dead bird fell out of the sky. And I knew: it was the beginning of the end. I had to quit being Mole King immediately. And I had to do it spectacularly, so that the Moles all took it seriously.

I followed it up by swearing that they'd never see my face down in the Mole realm ever again.

I was never really meant to be the Mole King anyway. I was only made King by this lousy Mole named Croogy, so that he could use me as a pawn to instigate a war with the Slug People and cause giant worms to destroy the surface world. He forced me to do it by threatening to expose the embarrassing fact that I was Mole King to everyone at my school. Luckily I managed to defeat him with the help of my Royal Guard, and some Slugs, and some other creatures called Stone

Goons and Mushroom Folk. And this licorice-haired, ping-pong-eyed girl who sits near me in class named Magda. She's super weird, and won't leave me alone, so is not at all helping my goal to eliminate weirdness from my life.

Together we rescued the true Mole King, who Croogy had kidnapped, and put him back on the throne. But that guy immediately "abdicated" (which means he took off on a bike), and left me getting my neck bones crushed under the fifty-pound crown.

I'd finally left the crown back where it belonged. But the real problem was that there was an open grave in my backyard that led directly to the Mole realm. Moles popped out of it all the time. It was like that Whac-A-Mole game, except I didn't have a mallet, and my prize was I got to keep being the weirdest human in the Up-world.

It had become clear that I was never going to get out of being King of the Mole People as long as I lived next to a hole that led right to Mole People ground zero. The problem was that the

hole was in the backyard of a creepy graveyard mansion where I lived with my dad. And moving out of a creepy graveyard mansion comes with a built-in dilemma: *nobody wants to buy a creepy graveyard mansion.*

DREADSVILLE MANOR
(MY NICKNAME FOR IT)

HOLE FROM "BABY" MEGA WORM

BUSTED WEEDWHACKERS

ENOUGH BATS TO CHOKE A WHALE

We inherited the place from a relative, and we had to move in because our finances are what bankers kindly refer to as "nonexistent." My dad said he'd be happy to sell it if we could, but he hasn't so much as wiped a cobweb to help. I think he actually likes it here, and I think every day that goes by he and the house become more entwined.

So it was left to me to try to find someone to help sell it. But we found our mansion was what real estate agents kindly refer to as "you've got to be kidding."

I wasn't kidding, so I'd set to work using all the expertise and finesse I could muster to get the place looking polished and picturesque.

POWER SANDER

GRAVE-STONE

BAT POOP

But it seemed to resist all efforts of improvement. Every tombstone I patched seemed to re-crack. Every dead bush I tore out seemed to resprout. And no matter how much dirt I shoveled into it, that grave hole to the Mole realm just would not fill in.

The interior was no better. Peeling walls, stains that changed shape before your eyes, pipes that seemed to play old maritime shanties every time you turned on a tap.

The place was the physical manifestation of weird. It was going to be practically impossible to get it into a condition that someone, even if only a forlorn misanthrope, might want to buy. And I'd started to grow tired of trying.

Then: dead bird.

I was back on that sander in a flash. Hurling the crown was meaningless if I didn't get away from that hole.

Weirdness was picking up speed. I could feel it. Like it was trying to get my attention over the blaring sound of the power tool. I had a sixth sense about these things; I could detect abnor-malities beyond the scope of others. I focused my powers and let them point me in the direction of where it was emanating from.

Dang it, Dad!

If there was anything that might undermine your attempt to not be associated with weirdness more than your dad standing in front of you with a live eel trying to get your attention over the sound of your sander getting gummed up on bat poop, I don't know what it would be.

He was returning from the stream at the back of our property with a fresh eel that he'd just fished out. Oh, did I forget to mention? We have a stream full of eels in the back of our property. Gotta make sure to list that on the real estate feature sheet.

And with those eels, my dad began filling our pots, pans, pie plates, casserole dishes, and muffin trays. It had started as a way to save on our monthly bills. I was like, *Dad, maybe if you stopped buying so many cooking containers we could afford to eat pizza.*

But I couldn't deny my dad had a knack for preparing eels. He was so good at it that he'd published a book, which at first I thought was ludicrous. Who'd want a book of eel recipes? His opinion was that there were already plenty of cookbooks centered around more typical ingredients, but nobody was doing eels, and he believed being unique is better.

I thought that was nuts. But he's my dad, and despite his oddness he was a pretty great guy who was doing his best. So I was going to be a dutiful son, and support his goofy little book project, and even turn off the electric sander so I could hear what had got him so excited this close to dawn on a Monday morning. How bad could it be?

"Some folks from the local news are coming to our house on Friday to interview me about my book!"

"Aww, Dad, come on!" I screeched.

"Isn't that great? They want to see how I work, where I live . . ."

"Dad, please! We can't let them film this place! Everyone will see it!"

"Yes! Everyone will see it!" He beamed with his big teeth. "Won't that be terrific publicity for the book?"

"I'm trying to keep a lid on weirdness! The last thing I need is for everyone to see the full extent of Dreadsville Manor!"

It took me a second, blinded as I was by the horrifying thought of my personal gallery of weirdness being broadcast all over town. But it finally clicked.

Everyone will see it. Regular folks. Forlorn misanthropes. This could be my chance to interest someone in buying it! All I had to do was get things shaped up by the time they arrived on Friday! This was great! This was . . .

Impossible. What was I thinking? I hadn't made one bat-hair's width of progress in all the time I'd spent sweating. How was I going to get everything looking presentable in just four days? I'd need a whole army of workers to do that, an army of workers . . .

ready to do . . .

my bidding . . .

"What's 'Dreadsville Manor'?" asked my dad.

"Huh? Oh, nothing," I said, dropping the sander and taking him by the arm (and making a note to myself to stop calling our house by that name). "You're right! What was I thinking? A local news story will be fantastic publicity for the book. Tell them the Underbellys can't wait to see them on Friday!"

"Really? Oh . . . okay!" said my dad, almost dancing with excitement at my sudden change of heart.

I told him I could really use some eel frittatas for breakfast and waited impatiently as he shimmied happily into the house, dangling the fresh eel. The last thing I needed was him finding out about the Moles. He'd probably invite the whole lot of them to move in.

Eel frittatas are actually pretty amazing. Or at least my dad's are. He really did deserve to have a book about cooking eels. But my mind wasn't on food at that moment. I was too busy thinking about that army ready to do my bidding. It was the perfect solution!

There was only one hiccup.

I had to talk to Oog. Who was a Mole. Who lived in the Mole Kingdom.

I knew heading down to the Mole realm seemed like it was going backward from my plan to stop associating with weirdness. But it was dawning on me that if I played this just right, by the end of the week I'd be free and clear of weirdness once and for all. And besides, *this* was definitely going to be the last time they were ever going to see my face down there.

I checked my watch, then pulled off my sander goggles, dropped into the grave hole that would never fill in, and ran. I had thirty minutes to get to the Mole Kingdom and then get to school, and I could absolutely not be late. Being late for school was the scariest thing I could imagine. And I'd seen a Mega Worm the size of a steamship.

2

MOLE LEVEL, ONE LAST TIME

Running isn't something I like, or am good at. But being forced to do things I don't like and am not good at is the story of my life so far. Maybe one day I'll get to eat chocolate-covered pancakes or ride in a speedboat or do a cannonball into a pool of rubber balls. Things I assume I like, but what do I know? I've never had time to try them, what with all the Mole duties and being unpopular at school and running.

And if you think running isn't so bad, you're probably envisioning a nice sidewalk or grassy field on a well-lit day. Whereas, this particular Monday morning, I was running here:

The Big Cavern was the main area in the Mole realm. It was coated in luminescent clay, had a raised throne area in the middle, and was filled with caves, grub gardens, and, of course, Moles.

There's no doubt that charging into the Mole realm when you're trying to stop being the Mole King kind of sends a mixed message. It's even more mixed if, when you get there, you announce:

It's mixed still further when you're so out of breath from running that your announcement comes out sounding more like:

Oog was a member of my Royal Guard, and my best Mole buddy, even though he had a tendency to miscalculate "helping" me in the Up-world and to mistake my personal injuries for hilarious jokes.

My plan was to get in, give my Royal Guard my kingly order, and get out again before anyone took up any time with impertinent questions.

"Hey!" said a round Mole, standing near me. "Didn't you quit?"

"Quit?" I wheezed. "No (gasp) way (gasp) . . ."

"Yeah, you quit rather spectacularly," said the Round Mole. "Threw the crown down the stairs and everything."

"I think you (gasp) misheard . . ."

"No, you were quite clear. You said that if we ever saw your face down here again, it meant that all creation had frozen over and the sky had shattered and crashed into the sea."

"That was just an expression (wheeze)."

"King!" said Oog, finally making his way through the crowd. "Oh no! Up-world freeze over?"

"No, I was . . . I was just joking," I said.

"I knew it!" bellowed Oog, hugging the breath out of me. "I knew King not really quit! King so funny!"

"Oh, it was a *joke*," said the Round Mole. "I don't get it."

Ploogoo and Boogo appeared, who are the other members of my Royal Guard. All three of them had been awarded extra Os in their names for their heroic efforts in saving everyone from Croogy and the Mega Worms, but it had been decided that the system of having your status represented by the number of Os in your name was cumbersome (the former King Zoooooooooooooooog's sixteen Os being a prime example) and that everyone should just use the number of Os that felt comfortable.

OOG
BEST MOLE FRIEND

BOOGO
MASTER DIGGER

PLOOGOO
HEAD OF ROYAL GUARD

RANDOM ROUND MOLE
WHO I WAS STARTING TO DISLIKE

"Booooog!" said Boogo.

"Oh no, has the sky shattered and crashed into the sea?" asked Ploogoo.

"It was either just an expression or a joke, depending on the moment," said the Round Mole, looking at me. "Maybe stick to smacking your head on stalactites if you want laughs."

"Listen, I've decided to stay being your King, but only for four more days," I said. "Now, I don't have much time, but I need you to—"

"The King is back!" yelled Oog, and a shower of grubs rained down on me. Grubs are the Moles' primary source of food, and throwing them is meant to be a sign of respect. Although this became more dubious when the Round Mole threw some into my mouth.

"But only for four days—" I tried to make clear through a mouthful of grubs.

"Since you're here and still King, we might as well tend to some royal business," said Ploogoo, and he started reporting how the King of the Mushroom Folk was claiming I got his son hooked on ice cream, and was demanding I bring them more. Ploogoo was efficient that way, and as the head Royal Guard was the obvious choice for taking over the crown. The only problem was he was having a little issue with his personal confidence.

"He crying like a baby all the time," said Oog to me quietly.

"Are you discussing my personal life?" said Ploogoo.

"Of course not! It not all about you, Ploogoo," said Oog, then turned back to me. "He have three-day-old grub juice caked in corners of mouth, and blow nose on back of hand. He depressed because girl Mole with horn on head not like him the way he like her. King real ladies' man. King have advice?"

Ladies' Man? How blind were these Moles? I told them I didn't have time for anything like that at the moment. I had a *kingly decree* to impart.

When Oog heard I was about to make a decree, he thrust the crown toward my head, which I protested, but Ploogoo reminded me that kingly orders don't count unless I'm wearing the crown. So I let him put it on me, and felt the familiar crack and buckle of my neck bones.

"Good thing it's made of stone," said the Round Mole, "in case you want to throw it down the stairs some more."

I kept my lips pursed to keep out falling grubs as I told my Royal Guard to borrow a bunch of garden equipment from the Up-world: rakes, hoes, wheelbarrows, etc., and bring them, along with thirty Moles, to my backyard at sundown. The Moles all started shouting at once, everyone wanting to be included in an excursion to the Up-world. I told them they needed to keep super quiet on this mission—it was of absolute importance that they not be seen by humans.

And now, if they didn't mind, I had important business to attend to.

"King want tunnel to school?" said Oog.

"How did you know I was late for school?" I asked.

"Oog know all about King's schedule. We

Royal Guard! Boogo make tunnel get you right to school door."

"No! No more 'helping' me in the Upworld!" I said. "It always goes wrong and makes things worse! I can take the perfectly normal route out of the Mole realm back through the open grave, thank you very much! In fact, no following me at all! Stay completely clear of my life from this point forward!"

As I turned to go I saw Ploogoo wiping moisture from his eyes. At first I thought it was because of me quitting, but then I remembered about the girl Mole. I asked him about it, and he said he wasn't crying, he'd just been cutting onion roots. That was a relief.

But then I started doubting his onion roots story.

HONK!

BACK OF HAND

Whether I moved away from the Mole hole or not, these Moles were never going to stop pestering me about being King if they didn't have a replacement. But there was no way anybody was going to follow Ploogoo if he was blubbering like a newborn. I needed him to get his head together so he could take this fifty-pound neck-breaker off my head.

But what did *I* know about ladies? I'd heard all mosquitoes that bite are female. That was about it. Girls seemed to like Marco, the theater kid in my class who always wore a scarf. I suggested trying to style it up a little like Marco. Ploogoo wiped his tears and nodded. Maybe I was good with lady advice after all.

Okay, I thought, everything *is* in motion. By the end of the week I'd have both the mansion and Ploogoo in shape, and I'd be out. I took one last look at the Big Cavern, because *this* time was *definitely* the last time I was ever going to be down here.

"See you soon," said the Round Mole.

I was really not a fan of this guy.

"All hail King Doug!" the cavern rumbled as I charged off. I checked my watch as I rushed back up the tunnel, pouring out the grubs that had collected in my crown. I gasped at the time.

I'd met giant worms, slugs with spears, and extraordinarily furious mushrooms. But there was one creature that was even scarier to be on the wrong side of. A creature by the name of Miss Chips.

3

SCHOOL BUS

There was a rumor that Miss Chips once punished a student for chewing gum in class by dousing him with sugar and burying him up to his neck on an anthill. It was probably an exaggeration, but she gave you the feeling that something pretty close to that was possible.

Miss Chips didn't actually punish kids very often. It was one of the advantages of having a teacher who didn't care much about her job or trying to stay awake during class. But every once in a while she did care, and you never knew when it might happen. And when it did, she could level a glare at you that could melt paint off walls and make you believe the anthill rumor was nothing compared to what could go down.

So I was back to doing more of that thing I can't stand where you have to move your feet really fast and your heart threatens to explode.

At nine o'clock on the nose I stumbled into the empty schoolyard. I was in rough shape . . .

But at least the running was over.

Then I heard the school bus starting up in the parking lot. I'd totally forgotten: *it was class field trip day!*

The school bus screeched out of the parking lot and took off down the street. My lungs gurgled as I lunged after it, waving my arms wildly.

I was relieved when two faces in the back window turned and looked out. Then I went back to not being relieved when I saw the faces belonged to Ed and Ted.

ED
MY BULLY.
PURVEYOR OF
TAUNTS AND
INSULTS.

TED
MY BACK UP
BULLY.
SPECIALIZES IN
PROJECTILES.

They turned and yelled something to the driver, and for a moment I thought they were trying to help me. But then the bus started going even faster.

It was putting some serious distance between me and my faltering legs when it suddenly came upon big hole in the road and screeched to a stop.

I stumbled to the bus, panting madly. A sudden hole in the road? Oh, how timely!

"I know you did that, Oog!" I yelled at the hole. "I gave you a kingly order to stop helping me in the Up-world! It always backfires and ends up in embarrassment! *No more help, do you hear me?*"

I managed to wipe the blinding sweat out of my eyes and realized the hole was just a pothole. Then I saw the faces of my classmates pressed against the window, looking at me like I was a wiener dog with a bucket on its head. See? It always ends up in embarrassment.

"Not bad, Underbelly!" said Coach Parker as he opened the doors. "Looks like all that water-boy exercise is good for your pencil legs!"

His laugh met Ed and Ted's laughs in the middle of the bus and mingled like smoke signals. But all I could focus on at that moment was the fact that I was now officially late.

I stumbled onto the bus, prepared to meet my doom. The fact that there probably wasn't sugar and an anthill on board was slim comfort. I had complete faith in the most-fearsome-creature-ever's ability to innovate some other horrific torture using whatever was at hand. I turned toward the terrifying specter and braced myself for the worst.

A reprieve. For now. But who knew for how long? Miss Chips could have been in the midst of dreaming up elaborate punishments. Or, with a drool puddle that large, had perhaps been sleeping in that spot all weekend. It was hard to say.

The coach hit the gas and I lurched toward the seats.

And fell right on top of Magda.

Magda is the girl with the licorice hair and ping-pong eyes who helped me stop a war in the lower realms and prevent the eradication of everything we know. She's the only other human who knows about the Moles and all the other underground creatures. She lives next door to me in a cute little house that she rebels against by dressing like someone who communes with the dead.

She's been a real friend to me. But she's super weird. And with weirdness starting to circle like a dangerous vortex of destruction, I had to stay as far away from her as possible.

"You're the one who fell on me!" she screamed when I said this to her.

"It's happening, just like I warned you!" I screamed back. "I played with fire for too long! I've got to eliminate weird from my life before everything blows sky high!"

"Well, maybe you should start by not standing in the street yelling at potholes," she said, brushing stray grubs off me nonchalantly. "This weirdness-is-going-to-swarm-around-you-and-destroy-everything theory of yours is total bunk, Underbelly."

"Oh really?" I said. "Have you forgotten what happened last time weirdness spiraled out of control around me?" I pretended my arms were giant worms thrusting out of the ground and crashing onto the seats.

"You're just using this as an excuse because you don't want to be King of the Mole People!"

"Shhhh! Keep it down!"

"Relax, Underbelly," said Magda. "Nobody's interested in us."

I looked up to see a Binkette standing in front of us.

She was holding a clipboard, taking some kind of survey. Then, as if to prove Magda's point, she decided we weren't worth it and moved to the next row.

The Binkettes are the group of popular girls that orbit the head popular girl, Becky Binkey. Part of my big experiment to fit in—along with signing up for groups and offering people gum—had been developing a crush on Becky. Everyone else had one, so it seemed like a matter of routine. Not as routine was announcing it publicly, which got me heaped with ridicule and scorn.

"I guess you're done with the Mole King thing anyway," said Magda. "The Royal Guard told me about your spectacular resignation. I heard the crown smacked you right in the head!"

"That's not the takeaway from that announcement!"

Magda had no doubt learned of my quitting through her official role as the Human Ambassador to the Moles. The former King Zog (the guy who had sixteen Os in his name) had become a big fan of humans and had visions of Mole/human unity. Unlike me, Magda embraces weirdness and loves associating with Moles. So when Zog needed a Human Ambassador (before he abdicated off on a bicycle), she got the gig. I warned them that any human/Mole interaction was ill-advised. If movies had taught us anything, it's that if humans find out about creatures, they get really relentless about trying to capture them to perform experiments on and stuff.

I told "Ambassador Magda" that her news was out of date, and that I'd decided to be their King again for four more days so I could get my subjects to help fix up Dreadsville Manor for selling. She said that was "grossly irresponsible."

"You're the one who's always saying Moles can't risk being seen by humans!" she yelled.

"I'm a ticking time bomb!" I yelled back. "The forces of weirdness are descending! *A dead bird fell out of the clear blue sky!*"

There was a collective sucking in of breath from everyone on the bus. For a moment I thought it was because they were all in agreement with me about the seriousness of the dead bird. But then I remembered that nobody was paying any attention to us bottom dwellers, and that everyone was responding to a massive blunder. For a nice change of pace, the blunder had been made by somebody other than me.

The survey Binkette had finished polling the bus with her question—"*What should the color scheme be for the dance: black and white, or spring pastels?*"—and rejoined her cluster of Binkettes. The Binkettes were chirping about the upcoming school dance, the theme of which was "Springtime in Paris," and were engaging in some tonal acrobatics as they spoke to their glorious leader, Becky. They were doing their best to sound cheery, while at the same time casually hinting that the dance was this Saturday, and that some things that needed to be done weren't getting done, without implying that the things not getting done were in any way the fault of Becky, the one in charge of getting them done.

Becky spoke little, yet somehow still managed to convey that she was bored of having to always be in charge, and that nobody appreciated how hard it was to be in charge all the time, and that she wanted to quit and let somebody else do it.

The Binkettes, like everyone else on the bus, smelled a trap, and the loaded notion hung in the air untouched. Any reply, or any noise at all, would be treachery. Anybody with any sense could see that.

"I could be in charge," said a boy. And that's when everyone sucked in their breath.

It was Pennyworth. One of the Brainers. Seemingly not the brainiest one.

"I could be head of the dance committee," he said, gathering nothing from all the breath-sucking.

The Binkettes let him know the magnitude of his blunder by way of a series of hyper-sharp barbs containing phrases like "living joke," "nature's greatest mistake," and "Penny-barf," accompanied by the most unmirthful laughs ever pushed through raspberry lip gloss.

I think Pennyworth had a crush on Becky—a *real* one, like most Becky crushes—and his comment had been spurred by a momentary delusion that she might actually appreciate him for rushing to her aid.

But all it got him was a barrage of remarks about how he didn't have anything close to the taste, social skills, or understanding of what it was like to even dance with a girl, let alone be the organizer of a dance, and that it was possible he didn't even know how to properly put on his pants.

I was almost starting to feel sorry for him, when he decided he needed a place to dispense all the bile he'd just been soaked with.

As a Brainer, Pennyworth was one of my fellow rocket-club mates. But that was something he wanted fixed.

"You're a disgrace to the rocket club, Underbelly!" he yelled. "You've amassed a copious number of violations!"

Pennyworth said "copious" a lot. It's a really annoying word. Or maybe it got annoying because he used it all the time. It's a chicken-and-egg thing, I'm not sure which came first.

"Your grades are abysmal! And you don't even know how to spell 'wick'! I demand your immediate expulsion from the Accelerators! By show of hands, all those in favor—"

"I quit," I said.

"What?" roared Pennyworth. "You can't quit! We're kicking you out!"

"Too slow, Pennyworth! He beat you to it!" said Magda.

"Ha ha, the lame-oids are fighting!" laughed Ed and Ted.

"I quit the soccer team too," I said, and it was Ed and Ted's turn to roar "What?" and get laughed at. This was probably going to cost me, but I was on a roll and wanted to wipe clean all my mistakes at once.

"And I quit the theater group too! And I don't really have a crush on Becky Binky!"

That last one went too far. It was possible not everybody had a crush on Becky, but nobody'd ever been so bold as to state it. Everyone quickly pivoted back to their more comfortable berating target—me.

Pennyworth, trying to regain some lost ground with Becky, pulled me to my feet and told me to look at her, this vision of perfection, and then to stop looking at her, because my eyes didn't deserve to look at her, and my brain didn't deserve to have a crush on her. I pointed out that I'd said I didn't have a crush on her, which brought forth more insults and jeers, and contact with at least one half-full juice box.

Becky herself didn't look at me. When you're that popular you don't need to cast disparaging looks—you have others to do it for you. Pennyworth scowled at me. The Binkettes scowled at me. Marco scowled at me and flipped his scarf. Coach Parker asked what was going on and Ed and Ted told him I'd quit being the soccer team water boy, and Coach Parker scowled at me.

I slumped in the seat, wiping juice-box juice from my shirt.

"Risking the Moles getting seen by having them work on your house is irresponsible and dangerous," said Magda, joining the scowl parade. "I'm going to tell them not to do it."

"It'll only be at night!" I said. "Besides, I'm still King, and King outranks ambassador! So I order you to stay quiet."

"You sure give a lot of orders for someone who wants to quit being King."

"I'm quitting! In fact, I can promise absolutely and completely, *I am never going below ground again!*"

The bus screeched to a halt and Coach Parker opened the doors.

"Okay, we're here! Who's ready to explore some deep underground caves?"

4

CAVES

Needless to say, the fact that the field trip was exploring underground caves came as a surprise to me. Apparently it came as a surprise to Miss Chips too, as she forgot to bring any equipment for us to go into caves with. Coach Parker wondered if maybe they should cancel the outing if they didn't have equipment, but Miss Chips said there was no way she was coming back on another day, and to proceed with the exploration.

Coach Parker led us to this humongous hole in the side of a rocky mound that disappeared into darkness.

"Caves sure are smaller than when I was a

kid," he said. "When I was young we had serious caves. Well, get on in there, get an education."

"But we need ropes and lights and provisions!" said Pennyworth.

"For a dinky cave like that?" said Coach Parker. "Here, here's a provision." And he hurled a PowerBar into the hole. "First kid who brings that back to me gets an A."

One of the Brainers doubted the coach's ability to grant A's for a field trip.

We headed off into the tunnels. The deep, underground tunnels. *Sigh.*

The kids started making "scary" sounds that echoed off the cave walls, but they tapered away as we went deeper. I don't know why they were getting unnerved. They'd put lights with arrows every so often to let you know you were on the right track. Mole tunnels never came with anything so accommodating.

Eventually the kids' voices had fallen to whispers, and I realized I was leading the way. I heard a few comments wondering why I seemed so strangely at ease down here.

"Uh, hey, why am I going first?" I stammered. "It's not like I'm comfortable in caves or anything."

Then Ed and Ted pushed past me, saying, "Look at big man Underbelly!" and "Not good enough to be our water boy!"

Pennyworth saw an opportunity to piggyback on the jocks' bravado, and pushed past saying I was also not good enough for the rocket club, and Marco pushed past saying I was also not good enough for the theater (tossing his scarf over his shoulder, which slapped me in the face). But Ed and Ted out-bravado-ed the others and rushed ahead. We found them waiting at a fork in the caves, where a lit arrow pointed right.

I might have taken a moment to scan my co-bullies' comments for legitimacy, but I just wanted to get this over with. So I started down the right shaft with the others following behind me. But the tunnel soon became narrow and rocky and dark, and filled with the echoes of Ed and Ted's distant snickers.

"Those soccer jerks moved the arrow!" said Pennyworth.

"We heard that, water boy!" Ed's voice reverberated through the darkness.

"That wasn't me—" I began to say, but Ed and Ted started throwing rocks and yelling that it was a cave-in and to run, and everybody started screaming and pressing farther into the darkness. Magda was yelling for everyone to stop, but they kept flailing their arms and pushing into a pile and suddenly the ground below us gave way and I felt myself tumbling through space.

I landed with a "splat" on some rocks, and heard the grunts of other kids landing around me. Everyone's "Owwwww!"s turned to

"Ewwwww!"s when we realized the cave we'd dropped into was completely covered in slime.

Although we'd fallen deeper, we could see better because everything was covered in luminescent clay, like Mole tunnels. I wondered if this was perhaps some old part of the Mole realm, but I didn't see any evidence of Mole life. Just a big cavern piled with foot-long oval rocks.

A grab bag of my classmates had fallen in, some Brainers, some Binkettes, Marco, Magda, and Pennyworth.

"Becky! Where are you? Stand by me!" said Pennyworth, before realizing she wasn't with us. Looks like popularity protects you from misfortune. But I guess Pennyworth thought he might still get some good press from the Binkettes. He stood up next to them in a rough approximation of a chivalrous pose. "Don't fret, ladies! I'll protect you!" But his feet slipped on the oozy rocks and his legs shot out from under him into a painful split.

"Gee thanks, 'protector,'" said Magda. "But us poor defenseless girls don't need saving, especially from a puny-foot like you."

It was true, that guy had surprisingly tiny feet.

"Now, stay calm, ladies," said Pennyworth, trying to regain his footing. "Don't become hysteric—"

"*We're doomed!*" screeched Marco. "*We'll never get out of here!*"

"These jerks don't realize we've got nothing to worry about," Magda whispered to me. "The Moles will get us out of here."

"I don't think so," I whispered back. "I ordered them not to follow me anymore."

"Oog likes you too much to leave you on your own."

"*We're going to starve!*" cried Marco.

I offered him a piece of Juicy Fruit gum, saying it might have some fruit in it, but he batted it away.

"There's a strangely copious amount of ooze in here," said Pennyworth. "And theses rocks almost look like . . . *eggs*."

"They're just rocks, Pennyworth," said Magda. "Like the ones in your head."

Magda whispered to me that she had a plan. There was a small hole on the far side. She thought the two of us should crawl through it and make some noise to see if any Moles could hear us. I was feeling pretty uneasy about the growing weirdness of the situation, but grumbled "Fine."

Magda told the others to wait here while we searched for a way out.

"You guys are heroic," said one of the Binkettes. "Underbelly is saving us!" said another.

"What? Underbelly's not going to save us!" said Pennyworth. "*I'm* going to save us!" Then his tiny feet lost their grip on the rocks and he did a leg split again.

"Stay here and work on your gymnastics routine," said Magda. "We'll handle this."

We made our way over the oozy rocks to the hole. There was a big rock in front of it, but enough space for us to squeeze through.

The tunnels on the other side were even more oozy. We couldn't even stand up and were reduced to lying on our stomachs and dragging ourselves like baby turtles on a beach.

"Hey, we can't yell for the Moles, the others will hear," I said.

"Just make loud noises then," said Magda. And we both started screeching like parrots. Then we lay there, listening to the sounds of our shrieks fading down the tunnels.

"Y'know, we really could die down here," said Magda.

"No way!" I said. "There's *no way* I'm dying in an underground tunnel! I gotta get out of here quick!"

"Oh right," she said, "you have to get home and make your innocent subjects do a bunch of yard work before tossing them aside like used gum."

"You still don't believe me that weirdness

is snowballing around me? Just look where we are!"

"It's not weird to get stuck in a cave, Underbelly. It happens to people all the time."

"What about those eggs?"

"They were just rocks!" said Magda. "Quit trying to make something more out of it than it really is! You are not a 'weirdness magnet'! There's no such thing!"

Before I could respond, we heard a sound. Something was moving toward us.

"See?" said Magda. "I told you Oog wouldn't leave you on your own."

But it wasn't Oog, or any Mole.

It was Slug People.

There's no way to sugarcoat it: Slugs are gross. Being repulsed by them is a normal reaction for anybody. Factor in the additional trauma of being threatened and imprisoned by giant ones, and the repulsion can easily become so great that you could find yourself barely able to breathe or speak in their presence. Certain words, however, are so important to say, that

SLUG PEOPLE!

even under such debilitating circumstances, you'll somehow dig deep and muster up the strength to say them.

"I told you so," I said to Magda.

"This still doesn't mean you're a weirdness magnet!"

"It totally does! People go into caves all the time! I'm the only one who runs into giant Slugs!"

The closest Slug scrutinized us with his eye-stalks. These weren't the first Slug People we'd met, but these ones were different. Thicker, slimier, and with angry eyebrows.

"Talk to them!" I whispered to Magda. "You're an ambassador!"

"You're King!" Magda whispered back. "King outranks ambassador—"

"Humans?" said the closest Slug, and the rest grumbled and burped.

"Uh, greetings," I said. "You guys haven't seen any Moles around here, have you?"

"Moles?" said the Slug. "Of course not. This is Slug People domain. We don't allow snooty Moles around here. Or humans, for that matter." He glided closer, stalks pointed down at us. "Why aren't you scared?"

I hated to burst his bubble, but not only had we met Slug People before, we'd also met a bunch of other creatures that resided on different levels below the surface. It went something like this:

And of all the ones we'd met so far, the Slugs were definitely the slimiest and grossest and most disgusting.

"Admit it. You humans find us slimy, gross, and disgusting!" said the Slug.

"Whaaaat?" I protested. "Not at all. You guys look great. Way nicer than that other group of Slugs we met. Sturdier. And your eye-stalks, so much less beady."

"You mean there's another tribe of Slug People?" said the Slug.

The Slugs looked at each other and burp-grumbled.

"That might have been too much information," whispered Magda.

The first Slug oozed forward till it felt like he was going to ooze right over us, slime seeping from around his gelatinous body.

"What are you even doing down here?" he asked menacingly.

"They with me!" said a familiar voice, and we twisted our heads around to see Oog appearing—as Moles like to do—from the shadows. The Slugs all bristled and made disdainful noises.

"He Mole King, and she Mole Human Ambassador!" said Oog.

"Mole King?" scoffed the Slug. "How could a human be a Mole King?"

"Don't get too surprised," I said. "I was only made King because of this stinker Mole named Croogy who made a deal with the other Slug tribe that if they helped him get rid of the old Mole King he'd let them take over the Mole level, because he wanted to take over the Up-world level. But he ended up betraying everybody. Luckily it all worked out, and we tossed Croogy down to the Mega Worm level with a bucket and a mop."

"Is that so?" said the Slug.

"Again, dude, TMI," whispered Magda. I guess that was one of the side effects of having so little social experience: I had a tendency not to realize when things shouldn't be said.

"You Slugs seem busy," said Oog. "Oog just get these two out of your hair. Or, not *hair* . . . you know what Oog mean."

And Oog picked us up one under each arm and started struggling over the ooze rocks, our bodies jiggling as he slipped and lurched. The Slugs seemed too surprised to do anything. Even their burping had stopped.

Oog carried us into a tunnel and then dropped us and started digging into a wall.

"I thought I told you not to follow me!" I said.

"Oog not follow," said Oog. "Oog just passing by, hear birds screeching. Oog think: What parrots doing down here underground?"

"How about being grateful?" Magda said to me. "He just saved us!"

"You just lucky they not realize you were in sacred egg chamber," said Oog.

"See? *See?*" I flailed at Magda. "It doesn't get any weirder than a chamber packed with giant Slug eggs!"

"Make sure you not touch any. Slugs got no sense of humor about their eggs." Oog broke through the wall, then spoke quietly.

"Okay, tell other kids come through here, then you all follow Oog up this way. Oog keep out of sight."

The small hole Oog had dug poked into the side of the egg chamber. I called my classmates and they carefully made their way to us, Pennyworth doing splits about six more times. They all squeezed through and followed us up the tunnel Oog had just taken. We found a freshly dug hole at the top that led back to the cave with the lit arrows and the rest of our class, where a happy reunion took place.

Everyone was bubbling as they filed up to the cave entrance and back into the light. Before I stepped through myself I felt something hit me in the shoulder. I turned and saw the PowerBar the coach had told us to bring back, and Oog smiling in the shadows.

"Just happened to hear bird screeching, huh?" I said.

"Yeah! Oog just happening by! Maybe Oog always just be happening by when King need help."

I smiled.

I turned away, then turned back. "But what if I'm no longer your King—" I started to say, but Oog had returned to the shadows.

I guess I was more accustomed to the sharp transition of dark caves to blinding daylight than the others. I was able to lead everyone back to the bus, where Coach Parker stood with Ed and Ted. We were all parched and begging for water.

"Sorry, water boy, they got the last of it," chuckled the coach. Ed and Ted belly-laughed with well-hydrated throats at our disheveled appearance and ooze-covered clothes, their own clothes drenched from having just finished a water fight.

"How thirsty could you have got from exploring that dinky little cave?" said the coach. "Back in my day we'd climb a whole mountain and never whine about water once."

Magda grabbed the PowerBar I had in my hand and held it up to the coach's face.

"You owe Underbelly an A."

The coach grabbed the bar, opened it, and took a bite.

"There's no such thing as giving an A on a field trip."

Miss Chips woke up as we climbed onto the bus, roared for the coach to get the motor started, and rolled over in her seat. The Binkettes were chirping extra loud, and I heard my name a few times. They were telling the others about their ordeal after falling through to the lower cave, and how it was me that got them out.

The bus was starting to get manic. All the pent-up anxiety from the caves was translating into volume. The coach yelled to pipe down, but nobody listened. Everyone was too pumped up about caves and possibly from dehydration, and from talking about me. I heard some backhanded compliments about how I was relaxed in the tunnels because of my similarity to worms, but I also heard one or two front-handed compliments. I even heard the word "hero."

"What do you know, Underbelly?" said Magda. "Looks like you're a *hero*."

I started to sweat. I knew better than to think this was a good thing. I knew that even if it was a positive ride for a while, it would eventually blow up in my face.

"If Underbelly is such a hero, why doesn't he take over as head of the dance committee?" said Becky.

The blow-up was faster than expected.

The bus erupted in a variety of sounds: snorts of laughter, snorts of disbelief. I guess it was mostly snorts. But Becky didn't follow up with a laugh, so the Binkettes had no choice but to take the comment as if it were real. Becky said, "All those in favor of Underbelly being the new head of the dance committee?" and everyone went along with what seemed to be the will of the most popular person in school, and yelled "Aye!"

"I can't be in charge of a dance!" I croaked. "When I'm in charge, terrible things happen!"

Magda was looking at me with that

knowing smile she does that I can't stand. "You're head of the dance committee! Ha! Good luck, 'hero.' I wouldn't be caught dead at one of those things."

"Neither would I!" I said. "I'm on a mission to *stop* being the head of an unruly mob! I don't want to be the head of another even wilder one!"

I took a peek over the seat behind me. Binkettes were staring at me like I was a herald from a parallel universe. Ed and Ted were looking at me like they were planning on grinding my bones to make bread. Marco was yelling about ooze ruining his jacket and mussing up his hair.

Even Becky was looking at me. As you may expect, when someone who never makes eye contact with you suddenly does, it can be very powerful.

She was saving her ignoring for Pennyworth, who was once again making a misguided attempt to impress her. For some reason he thought she'd be interested in rocks. He was trying to show her this strange one he'd brought back from the cave. It was about a foot long. And oval.

5

TWO MOBS

Backyard—Monday

So now I was in charge of two mobs: a bunch of
Moles doing landscaping, and a bunch of kids
putting on a dance.

Want to know two things I've never done in
my life? Done landscaping or gone to a dance.
I've also never put straws up my nose, worn a
hula skirt, or rocketed to Mars. What groups
would they put me in charge of next?

I had to assume that by tomorrow everybody
would be treating my appointment on the dance
committee the same way they'd treat a monkey
having won the presidency after too many people

voted for him as a joke: they'd all just laugh and give him a banana. I doubted I'd get a banana out of it, but I'd accept the laughs if it meant I was free to climb back up my tree. With any luck I'd meet up with Principal Wiggins first thing in the morning and get the whole hilarious episode wiped from the books before I had to endure any ridicule or fruit.

But that would have to wait. The school bus had returned to the schoolyard and released us back into the world, and I needed to get home and deal with my more pressing concern: the impending arrival of news cameras at my house on Friday. Dreadsville Manor had to be transformed in four days. Because if it wasn't, my full weirdness and the house's full un-sellability was going to get broadcasted to everyone in a hundred-mile radius.

So it was with significant anxiety that I stood in front of the open grave in my backyard and watched the sun ease its way below the horizon. Then I waited some more. Then some more.

Finally I poked my head into the grave hole, and saw Oog standing at the head of the tunnel packed with Moles holding garden equipment and keeping incredibly quiet.

WHAT ARE YOU DOING?

"Is sun down?" said Oog. "We can't tell from down here."

I put on my crown and ordered them to start working, and the Moles began piling out of the hole with their equipment.

I directed them to various jobs: scrubbing stones, pulling weeds, filling in holes, and fishing dead bats out of anywhere they found them. I told them to dig up a bunch of living trees and shrubs and grass near the back of the property and replant them in more visible places. I told them to hide my dad's eel-catching equipment by the stream.

Work didn't move fast. Most of the Moles hadn't spent much time aboveground, so were distracted by fascinating things like stars, or wind, or insects that had the audacity to fly instead of crawl.

They were noisy too. They kept stepping on rakes and smacking themselves in the face, or dropping heavy objects on each other's feet, like one of those old black-and-white movies featuring a group of inept brothers that only grown-ups found funny. "Quiet!" I kept hissing.

Ploogoo was even more distracted than the others. He stood wearing a scarf and watching the female Mole with the forehead horn admiring the garden, even though much of it was outright dead. I guess when you live underground any vegetation looks good. I ripped up some wildflowers, pulled off his scarf (this just in: scarves don't work on Moles), and shoved the flowers into his hands.

"Here," I said. "Give her these."

"These? Are you sure?" said Ploogoo.

"Yes, they're flowers, they'll work," I said, with more confidence than I really felt. I of course had no firsthand proof of the power of flowers, but I assumed all the flower stores I'd seen around stayed in business for a reason.

The female Mole took the bouquet, looked at Ploogoo like this was a sick joke, and dropped it in the mud.

SPLAT

Ploogoo returned to me, the lines of his brow and mouth flattened beneath the weight of yet further crushed confidence, before rising slightly as he remembered a piece of official royal business. He informed me a new tribe of Slug People had found the Slug tribe that resided below the Moles. They were a different type of Slug, "Bull Slugs," in contrast to the "Common Slugs" we already knew.

"Nobody knows where they came from or how they became aware of the Slugs below us," said Ploogoo.

I cleared my throat, and Oog did as well, to show me that he'd kept quiet about our little encounter.

"They're bigger and slimier than the Common Slugs," said Ploogoo, "and their burping seems more nuanced and complex—"

"No time for that," I interrupted, tossing him a shovel.

We worked through the night. It was hard for me to see the progress in the limited light, so I had to rely on the Moles' superior night vision.

But really, it was just planting. How much could they mess that up?

Turns out a lot, which I only realized when the first rays of light fell across the trees, bushes, and grass that had all been planted *upside down.*

For Moles, the visually appealing parts of plants are the beautiful roots that grow from their ceilings, while the leafy parts that protrude upward are, to them, the ugly roots. This explained why they were so enamored with a garden that was filled with rootlike dead branches. And why the forehead-horn Mole had been so unimpressed by Ploogoo's "flowers."

I looked around at the disaster of my yard. End of night one, and we were further behind than when we started.

School—Tuesday

The first thing I did upon arrival at school was go to Principal Wiggins's office to deal with the hilarious dance committee joke. I got there with horribly perfect timing.

My eyes were throbbing from lack of sleep. I should have been treating them gently, and not forcing them to look at things that eyes were never meant to see.

Principal Wiggins, attempting to scold Miss Chips.

He'd heard about the fiasco of the field

trip to the caves. How she'd forgotten to bring equipment, how she'd let the kids enter the caves unsupervised, how they'd gotten lost and how they might be lost there still if one heroic child hadn't saved them.

I willed my frozen body to back me away, but when I moved my neck it cracked (from wearing the heavy Mole crown all night).

"That boy right there!" he said. "He saved the other students! They were so thankful to be alive that they made him head of the dance committee!"

"About that—" I started.

"With Becky in charge, we could count on everything going fine," said Principal Wiggins. "But with this Underbelly kid, who knows what could happen? That's why . . . that's why . . ."

Miss Chips looked up, sensing what was coming. Principal Wiggins faltered. Then forged ahead.

"That's why I'm putting you in charge of this Saturday's Springtime in Paris dance!" he declared. Miss Chips growled like a bear hit with a tranquilizer dart. "You will work alongside Underbelly. You'll supervise both the decorating and the event itself. The two of you will be in charge . . ."

Her gaze intensified. I couldn't help but wonder if Wiggins was going to get out of this without being buried up to his neck on an anthill.

". . . together," he croaked, and slumped onto his chair.

"Paris?" said Miss Chips, which was the only word she said.

Then she turned her gaze on me. It was already warmed up from being used on the Principal, so it reduced my insides to pudding. Fortunately she must have been late for a nap or an armed conflict or something, because she got up and left the office. I think her laser-gaze skimmed over the bulletin board as she went by, because thumbtacks popped from the cork and papers fell to the floor. Wiggins and I looked at each other with the sweaty stares and heavy breaths of fellow shipwreck survivors clinging to debris on a beach.

MELTED PAINT

POPPED BOW TIE

FALLEN PAPERS

"Principal Wiggins," I stammered, "about the dance committee . . ."

"Don't worry if you've never danced with a girl before, Underbelly."

"No, it's not that—"

"Your fellow students have honored you

by giving you this position. Over Becky Binkey, astonishingly. And frankly, you don't have the social currency not to accept. Besides, I've already given Miss Chips the assignment to work with you." He sighed. "I'm not going through that again."

By the time I got to the classroom there was already a thick layer of disgruntlement in the air. Miss Chips had announced she'd been made supervisor of the dance. And just so there was no doubt how she felt about it, everyone had to write a five-thousand-word report on plate tectonics. Even the Brainers only knew a couple hundred words about this subject at best, so we were expected to just write "plate tectonics" over and over till either we reached five thousand words or our hands had broken and our fingers had fallen off.

The class was grumbling and looking for someone to take it out on.

"Blame him," said Miss Chips, pointing at me.

And they did.

FREE
BANANA
AFTER ALL

Backyard—Tuesday

Again the sun went down, and again I donned my crown and watched my subterranean cleanup crew bubble from the grave hole for another long night of work.

Before I'd run off for school that morning I'd given the Moles a picture torn out of a gardening magazine to show them the kind of thing humans liked in a yard.

Oog and Boogo came out of the hole smiling broadly, telling me to trust them, they'd figured it out, and knew exactly what to do to get the yard looking like the magazine. I quickly checked the back of the page to make sure there wasn't an ad for wrecking balls on the other side or something. Moles are very literal. But they assured me they knew what photo I wanted.

While we worked, I took a moment to apologize to Ploogoo for sending him to his Mole lady with flowers the wrong way up.

"It wouldn't matter," said Ploogoo. "For

what earthly bouquet could but wilt 'neath the beauty of my sweet, fair Lindoog?"

"SHHHH!" I hissed to Oog and Boogo as they knocked down a tombstone while trying to tie a hammock to it. Then to Ploogoo, "Hey, what you said there gives me an idea! You should recite her a poem!"

"Really? You think she'll like that?" said Ploogoo.

"Yes, it's poetry, it'll work," I said, again with more confidence than I felt. I had no firsthand proof of the potency of poetry, but I assumed all the greeting card stores I'd seen around stayed in business for a reason.

Not much rhymes with Lindoog, so I came up with this:

> *"Roses are red,*
> *Violets are blue,*
> *Mud is brown,*
> *And so are you."*

He asked if I was sure about this, and I said yes, shoving him forward.

The sweet, fair Lindoog listened to Ploogoo's poem, and turned and walked away. I shook my head. Ploogoo must have been terrible at reciting poems.

The Moles worked through the night, and even in the limited light I could see everything around me taking on a sparkly, magical glow. "This is looking great!" I said.

Which I guess was too much for Captain Bring-down Ploogoo, because it set him off babbling about the giant Slugs again.

He started telling me how the Bull Slug Ambassador, whose name was Gurge, was putting the pressure on the Slug Ambassador that we knew, whose name was Sputz. I commented that Slug names all sounded like embarrassing body noises. Ploogoo told me the Bull Slugs knew about the deal the Common Slugs made with Croogy to kidnap the old Mole King (King Zog) in exchange for some real estate on the Mole Level, and Ambassador Gurge was asserting that since the Common Slugs kept their part of the bargain, the Moles still owed them big-time.

"Nobody knows how these new Bull Slugs found out about the deal with Croogy—" said Ploogoo.

"Ahhh! This is a disaster!" I yelled.

"Well, it's troubling, yes, but I think maybe we can talk to the Slugs and—"

But I wasn't talking about any Slugs. I was talking about the yard, and my latest, even more massive mistake. As the first rays of light fell across the trees, bushes, and tombstones, they revealed that the Moles had covered everything with *luminescent clay*. The photo I'd given them was, of course, taken in daylight, so they assumed I wanted the yard to be more well lit. In darkness, luminescent clay has a pleasant glow. In the light, it just looks like clay. Clay that's the color of . . . I don't even know, it was indescribable.

"King like?" said Oog.

"King not like!" I said. "It's the most unattractive color in the history of eyeballs!"

"Color?" said Oog.

Turns out that Moles are colorblind. Which makes sense for a group of creatures that live their whole lives underground. And might also explain why reciting a poem about color to a girl Mole would be poorly received.

End of day two—the yard was covered in upside-down foliage, and caked with clay the color of baby poop excreted from a baby that had eaten nothing but mustard. There, I figured out how to describe it.

6

MIDWEEK

School–Wednesday

So being in charge of the Moles was going as disastrously as usual. Let's see how being in charge of the dance committee was going.

Miss Chips had made it clear she wanted all the decorating she was supposed to be supervising to be finished by Friday, as there was no way she was coming in on Saturday prior to the dance.

Work was done after class, presumably during a time Miss Chips was usually at home eating marshmallows and watching game shows. Stuck instead at school, she brought a trash bag of marshmallows and a portable TV and set herself up on a folding chair by the door of the gym. She would then glower at me for a full thirty seconds to cauterize a warning on the inside of my skull—a warning I might keep in mind when making any reports to Principal Wiggins about her level of involvement—and then pay no further attention to the proceedings.

Besides me, the dance committee consisted of the three Binkettes, Marco, Becky, and Pennyworth. Despite having resigned as committee head, Becky stuck around to oversee things and make sure they were not going well.

And Pennyworth had joined to prove to Becky that he would have been a far better choice than me, which also entailed making sure things were not going well.

Pennyworth tried commiserating with Becky about how much I was going to mess everything up, and how Becky was clearly doing a great job that nobody appreciated.

The Binkettes and Marco were torn. The Binkettes were invested in the dance because it was a social event that underlined their lofty status. And Marco was invested in the dance because he had a new scarf from Milan he wanted to debut. But they were also keen supporters of me failing dramatically. It was a quandary for them.

Pennyworth took charge of the poster-making and tried to wreck everything by purposely misspelling "dance" on all the posters. But it turned out that "danse" was how you spelled "dance" in French, so it actually worked with the "Springtime in Paris" theme. So he just spilled paint on them instead.

Then we had to decorate the gym. Except Coach Parker was running a floor hockey practice in there and refused to relinquish any space. Little plastic pucks kept connecting with heads. They said it was accidental, but I couldn't help but wonder if that was true, since the heads the pucks connected with were pretty much only mine and Pennyworth's, and Ed and Ted and the Coach kept laughing and yelling "bull's-eye!"

I had to hand it to Ed and Ted, their floor hockey skills were pretty sharp.

The pucks also accurately knocked over cans of springtime pastel paint and tore through streamers we were trying to hang. One got stuck in a big papier-mâché croissant and the whole hockey team bashed it to bits with their sticks, saying they needed to "play it where it lays."

One of the Binkettes suggested that, for the "springtime" part of "Springtime in Paris," we should get loads of leaves and tape them to the walls, but this was shot down as something that would take hundreds of hours to accomplish and divert too much time away from the decorative centerpiece of the event: a replica of the Eiffel Tower.

The tower was something Becky had suggested while she was still reigning, and she and the Binkettes seemed to like the idea even more now that it could be blamed on someone else if it failed.

The proposed size of the tower quickly escalated as kids giddy with lack of accountability kept one-upping the dimensions. The groundskeeper—who, like everyone, had a soft spot for Becky—provided a huge pile of metal rods from some old football bleachers, and we began laying them out on the gym floor after the floor hockey was finally done.

I questioned if it was going to be too tall to stand upright in the gym, and Pennyworth insulted my math skills for not being able to subtract a horizontal number from a vertical number. He looked at Becky and laughed at me. And Becky actually smiled. So apparently I did have some ability to help create romance. I just had to get Ploogoo to insult my math skills in front of Lindoog, and the sparks would fly.

There were a few hours between the

time Miss Chips swatted us with her empty marshmallow garbage bag to get us to leave and the time the sun went down. I might have used this time to catch some sleep, but instead I dragged a bunch of bags to the collection of trees behind the science portable. Magda found me there, filling the bags with leaves.

I'd been avoiding her because I had the feeling she still wasn't keen on me using the Moles for manual yard work. I got that idea because she'd been tossing notes on my desk like this:

"How's being King of the Dance Committee?" she asked.

I said it was terrible, because just like I told her, the weirdness was causing nothing but catastrophe.

"Look at all these welts on my head from floor hockey pucks!" I yelled.

She said there was no reason to blame any new influx of weirdness, as I'd been getting injured by random objects all year long. I asked her to give me ten examples, and she listed them quickly. I asked for ten more.

"Ever stop to think it's just 'cause you're a doofus?" she said.

"I am not!" I said, as my rake caught on a trash bag and ripped it, spilling leaves back onto the ground. "See? One minute it's a ripped trash bag, and the next it'll be the destruction of everything!"

"You're just using this as an excuse because you don't want to be King anymore."

"I never wanted to be King!" I said. "Because I'm bad at it!"

"You're not that bad at it. Other than maybe you don't know when to keep your mouth shut," she said. "Speaking of which, have the Moles mentioned the new Slugs that you blabbed to? I wonder if they found out there were humans in their egg chamber?"

Ugh, right, that egg Pennyworth took. It's not like I wasn't concerned about that. I was. But with all those eggs down there, could the Slugs have missed just one? Once all this stuff with the house and dance and Moles was over, I'd make a point of finding it and taking it back underground. Even though I'd be completely finished with weirdness by then, I'd still do it. Because I'm that nice a guy. I wondered where Pennyworth stashed it. Maybe in the science portable I was standing next to. I'd check there next week.

"I don't have time for any below-ground affairs," I said. "News crews are coming Friday morning to film my house. Before then I've got to repair the carnage done by colorblind landscapers, create Paris in a gym with a committee bent on my destruction, and try to keep Miss Chips's eyes from boring a hole into my skull. But just a few more days and then I'll be out! Done! Never in charge of anything again!"

"And you're doing all this," said Magda, "being irresponsible with your authority, putting the Moles in danger of being seen, trying to shirk the honor bestowed on you by a group that calls you friend . . . all because a dead bird fell out of the sky?"

"Well, yeah," I said. "That, and avoiding looking weird. Don't think I'm okay with everyone thinking I'm a weirdo just because I accepted being seen with you."

Magda's ping-pong eyes narrowed to slits.

"One day," she said, "when you're grown up and you're doing some boring job surrounded by people who jog on treadmills and file their taxes and stare at computers all day, you'll realize this was the most amazing experience that was ever offered to you. And you squandered it."

The rake ripped the bag again. I turned to show her how un-amazing this experience was, but she'd already walked away.

Backyard—Wednesday

The Binkettes' idea of taping leaves onto things had stuck in my head. Even better than on walls, it could be used on trees. Getting an entire gym covered in leaves using only a handful of surly, uncooperative dance committee members? Never gonna happen. But getting a yardful of dead trees covered using a large group of underground dwellers ready to do your bidding? Game on.

10 BAGS OF LEAVES

40 ROLLS OF TAPE

EEL JUICE AND EEL CHIPS FOR SNACKS

I had ten bags of leaves waiting for them when they spilled from the grave hole that night, and I set them to work scrubbing off clay and taping leaves.

I saw Ploogoo approaching, and hoped he didn't want any more tips on impressing girls, because I was out. But instead he had his own brainwave. "What about compliments?" he asked. "Do girls like receiving those?"

I shrugged. But I told him he might as well give it a try. Looking at Lindoog, I wondered what stood out about her that he could compliment. There was that big horn sticking out of her forehead. I told him to try complimenting that, see what it did.

Well, it didn't do much, other than cause her to storm away from him again. I was realizing my complete lack of interaction with girls all my life had left me with a pretty gaping hole in my understanding about them.

The night wore on, filled with the sounds of my yawns and of Moles taping leaves and digging and scrubbing and not even really stepping on rakes all that much. The eastern sky began to brighten, and I flinched in anticipation of what latest catastrophe would soon be revealed.

But to my astonishment . . . things looked good! The clay was gone, and fresh leaves rustled on every tree and bush. Boogo had dug a pond and lined it with stones. Oog had created a natural canopy over the hammock. The unfillable open grave was camouflaged with bushes. The pathway wrapped through the grounds in the shape of the Celtic symbol of serenity. And there wasn't a dead bat to be found.

"King like?" asked Oog.

"King love!" I said excitedly. "King so happy!"

But that was Ploogoo's cue to commence talking about the Slugs again. He started by telling me about the King of the Bull Slugs, who was apparently huge.

"Much bigger than the King of the Common Slugs," he said.

This was relevant because Slug Kings earned their crown during a ritual called "The Great Slugging," where all the Slugs pile on top of each other and crush the ones below them. Hugeness is a clear advantage in this selection process.

"The Bull Slugs aren't just thicker and slimier," said Ploogoo. "They're more aggressive too. They want to merge with the Common Slugs and then confront us about the Croogy deal. They're demanding to speak with you, King."

How many times did I have to tell them that I wasn't going back down there, that I was abdicating being King?

"I'm starting to have strong suspicions that you guys never took my one-month time limit to find a replacement seriously!" I declared.

"Of course we not take it seriously," said Oog. "Our calendar only two rocks piled on top of each other. But also, you best King! We love you! Who else we get?"

I looked Ploogoo up and down. I couldn't help but feel my efforts to help him win Lindoog's affection and boost his confidence had been unsuccessful. The only improvement I could see was that he'd at least stopped blowing his nose on the back of his hand.

I pointed at him anyway because I didn't have anywhere else to point, and everyone turned to look behind him, including Ploogoo, before realizing who I meant.

"Me?" said Ploogoo, dabbing tears with the scarf. "Nobody would rumble for me during a Crown Rumble." The Moles who were filing past into the bushes that led back down into the grave hole looked over and shook their heads to indicate this was true. One made a raspberry sound.

A Crown Rumble was the Moles' less body-crushing way of selecting a king. They put the crown on the head of any prospective rulers, and whoever got the loudest rumbles won.

"But you're the better person for the job!" I yelled, and I really believed it, and not just because I was delirious from lack of sleep.

"All he needs is a vote of confidence! Come on, let's do the rumble right now!" I said, taking off the crown and holding it toward Ploogoo. "*Rummmmble!* Come on, Oog, join in!"

Oog gently pushed the crown over my own

head and then rumbled loud enough to be heard for blocks. I'd forgotten how loud Mole rumbles could be. Which wasn't surprising—I was so tired I could barely remember my name.

"Doug!" I heard my dad's voice call. Oh yeah, that was my name. "Wow, what a transformation back here!" I heard him say.

"Quick! Everybody out of here!" I whispered, and the rest of the Moles disappeared into the bushes surrounding the grave hole. Oog paused on the edge.

"Oog stand behind you, King. You our King!"

"Yeah," I said, "but what if I stop being your—?"

Oog popped out of view as my dad appeared, looking around at the new yard. "I hardly recognize it!" he said. "I sort of thought it had a certain charm the way it was. But I guess you thought it needed an update. You certainly worked hard on it." And then, seeing my face: "Maybe *too* hard. You don't look so great, sport!"

NOTHING COMPARED TO HOW I ACTUALLY FELT

"Don't worry, Principal Wiggins," I babbled. "Miss Chips is doing a great job supervising us . . . The decorating will be completed on time . . . There's nothing to worry about . . ."

"Sounds like you could use a good, nourishing breakfast," said my dad. "How 'bout some eel waffles with eel syrup!"

I told him that sounded great, but to make those waffles to go, because I had to get to class. He asked if I was sure I was okay, and I told him I was fine, everything was on track, there was no reason to worry about me whatsoever.

School–Thursday

I woke up at my desk with an eel waffle stuck to the side of my face.

You might think falling asleep in class would give me something in common with Miss Chips and mellow her out toward me, but no. She treated it like I was mocking her, and got so irritated she gave everybody a surprise test on photosynthesis. The waffle nap had done nothing to help my memory, and I got a zero on the test. Although I'm not sure I knew the answers anyway.

It was now Thursday, and Miss Chips had made it clear we'd better get all the dance decorations done before the end of the day, as she was tired of spending extra time at the school. So we did at least have that in common. I wanted to get home as soon as possible and start sleeping so that I could wake up well rested Friday morning and greet the news cameras with a smile.

All I needed was for everything to go perfectly smooth with the decorations.

I was so blurry-eyed with exhaustion that I

didn't register any concern at the final size of the Eiffel Tower, looking huge lying on its side on the gym floor. Or at the sight of a rope wrapped around its top, running out a window, and tied to the back of the groundskeeper's lawn tractor.

I also wasn't concerned when Principal Wiggins showed up and asked me to comment on the job Miss Chips had done supervising the committee. This time Miss Chips's cauterizing glare had no effect on me since my eyes were too closed for hers to make contact with.

"Don't worry, Dad . . . ," I babbled to Principal Wiggins. "The tombstones are straight . . . The bat poop is cleaned up . . . There's nothing to worry about . . ."

I wasn't even concerned when Pennyworth ran into the gym and started waving an object in Becky's face that was about a foot long and oval, saying "*Movement!*" and "*I was right! I was right!*" and boasting that after the scientist he'd called arrived to verify what a valuable find it was, he was going to be copious amounts of famous. Then he hoisted the object aloft and cackled like a villain from a bad movie. I think we were witnessing someone transform into a megalomaniac.

By then, through my bleariness, I was growing a bit concerned, because I realized what Pennyworth was holding was the Slug egg. If I'd understood him correctly, something inside it was moving, and he'd convinced some scientist to come examine it. The inherent flaw in my plan to put off taking the egg back to the Slugs suddenly became apparent: sometimes eggs hatch.

I needed to get the egg away from Pennyworth and back underground without any further delay. And to do that I needed a subtle, well-contrived plan to remove it from Pennyworth's possession.

REACH
REACH

My plan failed, and Pennyworth started mocking me. But he wasn't drawing from his regular material. He was saying he'd arrived in the science portable yesterday and had overheard me talking to Magda.

The bleariness parted, and I got worried for real. He'd heard me talking to Magda! He started telling everybody that Magda and I talked to underground men, and I thought I was their King, and I collected ten bags of leaves to give to them for some reason.

I thought I was sunk.

But everybody just kept doing whatever they were doing. Fortunately nobody takes what megalomaniacs say seriously.

"And he's got news cameras coming to his house tomorrow to film it inside and out and display it all on the news!" announced Pennyworth.

This, the kids got excited about. It was far less abstract than delusions of underground kingdoms. A straightforward chance to see all of a fellow student's weirdness dragged out into the light. But little did they know I had turned the entire grounds into a plain, normal, home-and-garden paradise.

But then I started feeling concerned again.

One little word Pennyworth had said. What was it?

"Inside."

With all the mess-ups outside, combined with mind-obliterating levels of sleep deprivation, I'd totally forgotten about Dreadsville Manor's *interior*!

It all came rushing to me at once: the shape-changing floor stains, the jars filled with eel jawbones, the wallpaper that dripped blood (or at least rusty water), my collection of space action figures (not necessarily deal breakers for selling a house, but not helpful for me personally).

What difference would the yard make if everyone saw all of that? I had to fix it! But there was no way I was going to get it done on my own by morning. I needed help! I needed my faithful subjects! I needed Moles!

Which meant . . .

Dang it!

Okay, one more trip to the Mole level. But *this* was *absolutely* going to be the *last time*! And after this, everything was going to be completely and totally *fine*!

"Go!" yelled Marco to the groundskeeper sitting outside on the tractor.

7

MOLE LEVEL, ABSOLUTELY LAST TIME

"**H**ey, it's King Quits-a-Lot again," said the Round Mole.

"Quit calling me that!" I said. "I'm just here to talk to Ploogoo."

"Oh no! Did I misunderstand *again?*" he said. "I keep believing you when you say we'll never see you down here anymore. Am I too trusting?"

"I'll be out of here in ten seconds. Ploogoo! *PLOOGOO!*"

"Gee whiz, I better stop being so naive. I'll never make it in this world if I continue being so gullible."

I really couldn't stand this Mole.

"Hello, King," said Ploogoo, barely looking up from an upside-down flower that he was absently picking pieces of root off of in a Mole variant of "she loves me, she loves me not."

Then he started in about the Bull Slugs again. I tried to cut him off, but he droned over me like a robot playing a prerecorded message.

Ambassador Gurge of the Bull Slugs was tired of being put off by the Moles. They wanted to speak to the Mole King immediately about compensation for the Croogy deal. Ambassador Sputz of the Common Slugs was trying to keep the peace, but Gurge was out of patience, and said that if the Moles didn't give them their due soon, the Bull Slug King was going to challenge the Common Slug King to a Great Slugging and take over both tribes, and then declare war on the Moles.

I told him that all sounded very important, but to get ready, because I needed him and one other Mole to meet me at the grave hole in half an hour for a super-secret, super-quiet mission. Ploogoo looked up at me with a sudden sparkle in his eyes, as much as Mole eyes could sparkle.

"That's it!" he said. "You mean for me to ask Lindoog, don't you? To feel needed, to be asked for aid, to be appreciated for personal talents . . . a girl would love that, wouldn't she?"

I shrugged. Whatever got him fired up to help with the job was fine by me.

"But King!" he said as I turned to leave. "What about the Bull Slugs?" He repeated some of the key words of the Bull Slug Ambassador, words like "demand," and "challenge," and "war." That last one was a real zinger. And then he mentioned my "diplomacy skills."

I said I was so tired I could barely stand up, and that this secret mission was our top priority. But not to worry. Even though I couldn't go meet with the Bull Slugs, I knew the perfect person to send in my place.

The curtains were covered with ducklings floating on a tangerine pond, and they hung in a back window of a house that looked like it was made of cake frosting, surrounded by a fence the very word "picket" was invented for, and bracketed by apple trees with apples so perfect no worm would dare pierce their skin.

The house belonged to my next-door neighbors, a couple who were right around the midpoint of raising a daughter whose aesthetics were in unexpectedly sharp contrast to their own. The ducklings had all been markered in with black.

I knocked on the window, and the ducklings parted.

"What are you doing here, Underbelly?"

I needed her help, that's what. Why else would I be here? "Nothin'," I said.

"Are you sure my weirdness isn't going to be too embarrassing for you?"

I said probably. Then I told her what Ploogoo told me about the Slugs, and repeated those zinger Bull Slug Ambassador words like "demand," and "challenge," and "war."

"That sounds serious," said Magda.

"The Slugs just want respect from the Moles," I said. "All they need is to feel heard, and have some sort of compromise figured out. It's no biggie."

"If it's no biggie, why don't you do it? Too busy feather-dusting your tombstones?"

I said I was. But she still didn't offer to help. I'd spelled everything out. What was she waiting for?

"So then . . . what is it?" she said. "What do you need?"

"Will you . . . help?" And boom! Just like that, she said she'd help! It was the wildest thing!

"But I'm not doing it for you," she said, squinting at me. "I'm doing it for the Moles."

"Great," I said. "If you get into any trouble, just call me on this walkie-talkie."

"Oh, so you're not going yourself, but you're ready to jump in with advice."

"Fine, don't take it."

Magda snatched the walkie-talkie. "In case I need you to fetch me some clean socks," she said with a grin.

I turned toward my house. Holy cow, was Ploogoo right? Magda seemed to like being asked for help, to feel like I needed her. What do you know . . . I guess I was smart about girls after all!

Maybe I should hit her with that appreciation *thing too*, I thought. I turned, but the pond of black ducklings had merged back together.

I found Ploogoo and Lindoog waiting for me at the grave hole. Lindoog didn't look overly impressed, but Ploogoo looked hopeful.

I had the crown with me and asked Ploogoo if it was necessary to wear it. He said technically it was, but he was willing to let it slide under the circumstances. I think Lindoog rolled her eyes.

I snuck them into the house.

"This place is amazing!" said Lindoog.

I didn't point out that Moles can hardly see three feet past their noses. If they had noses.

I pulled out some magazines to show them what regular humans liked to see in a home, and then pointed to the many, many things in my home that didn't match those things.

I said we had till dawn to get things looking as much like the magazines as possible. And we had to do it quietly. I'd convinced my dad to hit the hay early so he'd look his best for the cameras, and I promised I'd be doing the same.

But there was no time to sleep for me. Everything was riding on this. I was just going to have to pull up my socks, roll up my sleeves, and push through the night.

8

INTERVIEW

I awoke to the sound of knocking on the door, and Friday morning light spilling through the windows.

I'd fallen asleep! The blood-dripping walls—the shape-changing floor stains—the drapes that were more cobwebs than cloth! I hadn't taken care of anything!

The knock intensified, and I heard a woman's voice announcing herself and some station letters. I realized I was still holding the crown. I turned it upside-down and put a plant on it, then opened the door. There was no choice but to face the music.

They plowed in and started pointing their camera vigorously at everything. But each thing they pointed it at seemed to suck energy from their movements. The stains on the floor were gone. The walls were bloodless. The curtains and pillows and furniture had been cleaned and reorganized in a way that somehow transformed the whole place from haunted house to what the magazine referred to as "bohemian chic." Ploogoo and Lindoog must have worked through the night. And things looked great!

"Things look great!" said the reporter lady,

but she said it as an accusation. "First the front yard is all fixed up, and now the inside looks like just any normal old house!"

"Well, there's this plant holder. It's pretty outlandish," said the cameraman.

"This house was supposed to be weird! Where the heck is all the weird?" said the lady.

I was smiling to myself. They were too late. My home was officially normal. If they were on the hunt for weird, they were completely wasting their time.

That's when I noticed the window drapes.

COUPLE PAIRS OF MOLE FEET

HORN-LIKE BULGE

"Welcome to our home," said my dad, and the newspeople swung the camera toward him. The Moles might have de-weirded the house, but there was still my dad.

"Eagle to Squirrel," buzzed the walkie-talkie. "I'm here with the Moles, heading down to the Slugs."

The newspeople swung the camera at the walkie-talkie, then at me.

"Did that person say she was with moles, and slugs?" said the lady.

"I'm not the one you're here for! He is!" I said, pointing at my dad.

They turned the camera back on my dad's giant teeth and started asking him about bringing up his family in a graveyard. I shoved Ploogoo and Lindoog out of the curtain and into the hallway. The walkie-talkie crackled again as I pushed them up the stairs.

"I told you not to contact me unless it was an emergency!" I hissed into the walkie-talkie.

"No you didn't," said Magda. "Anyway, it's sort of an emergency. The Bull Slugs aren't happy that you sent me instead of coming yourself."

I could hear Ambassador Gurge yelling about how this was yet another insult to Slugs from Moles, and a round of burping assent from what sounded like a large gathering of Slugs. I told her only real, full-on emergencies.

"If you're really interested in seeing the whole place, I'd be happy to give you a tour," said my father, leading the news crew out of the living room. I ran up the stairs ahead of them. Two heads peeked out of my bedroom door. I hurried in and slammed the door behind me.

"What are you both still doing here?" I whisper-yelled. "Hey, this room looks really good."

"We decorated this one in 'Scandinavian Shabby,'" said Lindoog.

"She's so skilled at interior design," said Ploogoo, smiling at her.

"He got the idea to box up all those little plastic dolls," said Lindoog, smiling back, and they poked each other and giggled.

There was a knock at the door. "Sport? These folks are interested in having a peek in there," said my dad.

"Eagle to Squirrel!" squawked the walkie-talkie. "It's become a full-on emergency!"

"Not now!" I said, shoving Ploogoo and Lindoog into the closet.

"They've discovered one of their eggs is missing," said Magda. "And they remember seeing us outside the egg chamber. I told them they're bonkers if they think we know anything about any missing egg."

"Uhh, actually . . . I might know a little something about it."

"What??" yelled Magda. "You know about the egg?" An uproar of grumbles and burps swelled behind Magda's voice, and then, "Hey! Let go of me! Get your slimy appendages off of—"

And then I heard Magda scream.

More knocking. "What's going on in there, Sport?" said my dad. "We're coming in!"

My dad entered, followed by an excited news

crew, who looked crestfallen at the sight of yet another normal-looking room.

"I thought I heard a scream," said my dad.

"Oh, it's just Magda," I said, holding up the walkie-talkie. "She was laughing at a joke I told her."

Ambassador Gurge's fierce, guttural growl blasted forth. "I know where you are! I'm coming for you! And if you don't return what you took, I'll obliterate your entire world beneath an oozing wave of slime!"

My dad smiled. "I'm so glad you two have finally become friends."

The news people left to keep searching for something worth filming.

"Where are all your action figures?" asked Dad.

"They didn't quite fit the new 'Scandinavian Shabby' look I was going for," I said.

My dad asked if I was okay, and I wanted to answer, but I was frozen by the sight through the window of the shaking bushes around the grave hole.

He asked if I really didn't like living in our house as much as it was starting to seem, and I wanted to answer that too, but I was even more frozen by the sight of a giant Slug head peering through the leaves.

He asked me if I knew that the only thing that mattered to him was my happiness, and I really, really wanted to answer, but I was frozen rock solid by the sight of three giant Slugs oozing forth into our backyard.

Then I heard the news crew say the story was a bust, this place wasn't weird at all, and they should just check the backyard real quick and then split.

"Hey, you! Newspeople!" I yelled, blocking them in the hallway. "You came here to interview my Dad! Well, here he is! He's more interesting and has more talent than you can imagine! So ask him about his magnificent book of eel recipes, and do it right now!"

My dad looked at me proudly. The news crew sighed, pointed recording equipment, and started tossing questions.

"The secret to preparing eel is thyme," I heard him saying. "Both the sprig kind and the clock kind." And he laughed. Cooking joke, I guessed. But I was already down the stairs and into the backyard.

I wasn't far into the yard before I was on my butt. My feet had shot out from under me. The whole yard was completely covered in slime. I tried to stand, but it was impossible. Every-

thing was as slippery as . . . I can't even think of
anything as slippery as this was.

The yard was destroyed. Every surface was
slimed. All the leaves we'd taped on branches
were stripped off and the trees and bushes looked
dead in all-new shining and glistening ways.

And then I was surrounded by Slugs. Slimy,
revolting, terrifying Slugs. With hundreds of
pieces of tape stuck to their butts.

"Do you think we're a joke?" said the Slug

I'd met by the egg chamber, who I now realized was Ambassador Gurge.

"I can't believe the three of you managed to slime my whole backyard in five minutes!" I said.

"Compliments won't help you," said Gurge. "You humans are just like Moles! You think we're beneath you just because . . . well, we're beneath you. But we're not!"

"I understand what it's like to be on a lower rung," I said. "I was once ecstatic over getting the part of a shrub in a school play."

"You think we're gross and repugnant!" he said, oozing his gross and repugnant body forward and pointing an appendage at me. Slugs could elongate an appendage from the side of their body whenever they needed it. It was horrifying.

"No I don't!" I gagged. "You guys are adorable! I'd cuddle you and pet you if I could!"

"You think you can just come in and take one of our eggs? Well, now we've taken your ambassador. How do you like that?"

"No!" I yelled. I tried to stand up, but kept

slipping and falling down again. "As King of the Moles, I demand her release immediately!" It was hard to be demanding when lying in slime.

"King of the Mole People," he said. "You disrespect us by sending a subordinate! You ignore our demands! You steal our eggs! Ambassador Sputz and the Common Slugs may have put up with this kind of contempt, but the Bull Slugs are here now! We'll take the Mole level by force, if necessary! And if you don't give us the egg back, we'll take over this human level as well! Return our egg! You have twelve slime parsecs of time to do it."

"I have no idea how long that is."

"Just do it quick! Or we'll slime the human girl permanently!"

"Leave her alone!" I yelled, shimmying around in the slop and tape and leaves. But the Slugs had squeezed their bulbous, malleable bodies into the grave hole and were gone.

"I knew it! I knew we'd find weirdness!" I heard the reporter lady yell, and turned my head to see the newspeople running toward me from the side of the house, their camera pointing enthusiastically at a backyard dripping two inches deep in slime. "My journalist instincts never fail to—"

And then they were all sprawled in the slippery goo. Still, they never stopped smiling as they writhed about, filming, capturing the story of the weirdest house in town.

The Slugs had it all wrong. Your worth has nothing to do with what level you're on. I was on the surface, but lying there in the Slug ooze I couldn't have felt lower. I'd used my dad. Abused my role as King. Put my friends at risk. And got Magda captured by giant Slugs. And despite all this, my list of things to do—a mere two items long—was in shambles. *Sell the house?* My scheme to display it to the world looking palatable had failed completely. *Stop being King of the Moles?* I now had no choice but to find that Slug egg, grab the crown, and head back into the earth to try to fix a problem that was spiraling out of control because of me, even though all I'd ever tried to do was stay out of it.

It's like being Mole King was quicksand. The more I struggled to get free, the more it pulled me under. And now I had a ticking slime-parsec clock under me.

9

SLUG EGG

Did you know that slug slime doesn't wash off? Well, it doesn't, no matter how much you scrub it. It's resistant to water. I'd squirted squirts from every bottle in the bathroom, but still a thin layer of it remained everywhere ooze had touched skin.

After dragging myself through globs of the stuff back to my house and wasting time with an unproductive shower, I found Ploogoo and Lindoog still in my closet, where they were still busy complimenting each other on what a great job they'd each done on the house. At least I could claim one success. After flowers, poetry, and scarves, it turns out going through an ordeal together is the trick to bringing two people close.

I asked them what a slime parsec of time was, and Ploogoo asked if I was using a dry-mulch clock or a wet-mulch clock, and I said never mind. I gave them my backpack with the Mole crown inside it and told them to slide on their stomachs through the yard back to the grave hole and do whatever they could to stall the angry Bull Slugs while I went for the egg.

Annnnnnnd I was running again.

Finding the egg was easy. Like I expected, Pennyworth had stored it in the science portable, and I found it sitting in there on the counter. Unlike I expected, it turned out Pennyworth really had convinced a scientist to come examine it.

Okay, it wasn't a *real* scientist, it was just a science teacher from the nearby high school. But I suppose he probably studied some kind of science if he was teaching it, and he had those thick-framed glasses they must hand out to all the graduates at science school. He may not have been the kind of scientist who could call in troops of men with machines and weapons when they found a weird new life-form, but maybe he knew a scientist who knew a scientist who could.

I heard them approaching the portable, Pennyworth building up the "copious" amounts that life as we knew it would be changed by his discovery, and the science teacher grunting with the tone of one who'd been worn down. I was trapped!

I picked up the egg and felt little vibrations running through it. There was definitely something going on inside. As the door opened I had no choice but to resort to the most serious ninja stealth tactics.

Pennyworth shrieked when he saw that the egg was missing and started running around the room knocking things over. In the mayhem I stealth-ninja-ed out the door. When you're in full stealth-ninja mode, it helps to be covered in a thin layer of residual slime (I don't actually know if that's true, but for whatever reason I got away with it, so I decided not to overanalyze).

SCIENTIST GLASSES

NINJA

But whether the slime helped my stealth or not, one thing it definitely did was make holding on to things difficult. And dropping the foot-long oval removed once and for all any doubt about whether it was a rock or an egg.

The sound it made when it hit the ground was distinctly a CRACK.

I tucked it under my shirt and looked around. The last place I wanted to go was into the school. The school was where I'd recently failed to show up to Miss Chips's class, and left an Eiffel Tower embedded in the gymnasium ceiling. But there was no way I could get across the open field without risking Pennyworth exiting the portable and spotting me. The ruckus in the portable came to an abrupt halt, and I heard the sound of the portable door being kicked open by a tiny foot as I rushed into the school.

As I hurried down the hallway there were more cracking sounds from under my shirt, and a piece of eggshell fell to the floor. I heard the school door open behind me and I dove into the Principal's office.

From a stealth-ninja position in another garbage can (you don't realize how many garbage cans are around till you start hiding in them) I heard Miss Chips and Principal Wiggins butting heads over the abysmal state of the dance preparation, before they found a happy common ground in the conclusion that everything was all my

BITS OF EGGSHELL

fault. Because of me, Principal Wiggins was going to have to pay for a new gymnasium ceiling, a new gymnasium window, and a new lawn tractor. And because of me, Miss Chips was going to have to come in during the day on Saturday to oversee the completion of the dance prep.

They bumped into Pennyworth at the doorway, and I scrunched deeper into the garbage contents. I felt the egg cracking to pieces under my shirt, and the slickness of oozy Slug skin slithering against mine. I tried to stifle shudders of revulsion as Pennyworth and Wiggins and Chips all cursed my name before parting ways—three Underbelly-seeking missiles all armed and locked on me.

I climbed out of the trash can and hurried down the hall, then ducked into the gym. I knew there was an exit door on the opposite side of the gym, and there was nothing between it and me besides a huge Eiffel Tower crushed into the ceiling. Oh, and the Underbelly-seeking missile Miss Chips.

She was entering from the other door. I ninja-ed into a bin of basketballs.

Peering through the balls, I watched Miss Chips as she gazed at the mangled Paris decorations—the torn streamers, the bashed papier-mâché croissant, the crunched Eiffel Tower. Sure, a bashed papier-mâché croissant is pretty sad, but Miss Chips seemed gripped with a wistfulness and melancholy that went beyond ruined decorations.

She sat down in a chair beside the tower and began softly singing an out-of-tune song in French.

I felt some squirming around under my shirt and had to stifle a squeal.

The creature was doubtlessly trying to figure out what kind of bizarre shirt-world it had hatched itself into. I shuddered some more, hoping the basketballs weren't vibrating visibly. I was already starting to wonder how much more Slug I could handle, when an eye-stalk poked out of my shirt collar.

The familiar sound of Miss Chips's snoring came as some relief. The gym acoustics amplified the guttural noises nicely, and she followed each one with some mumbling about driving through the French countryside in a sports car with the wind in her hair.

WIND BLOWING FROM SOME-WHERE

I pushed the eye-stalk back down and pulled my collar tight. Then I felt the eye-stalks tickling around my neck and had to keep from giggling. I was going to have to secure this thing somehow if I was going to make it all the way back to the backyard grave hole without anyone seeing it. I crawled from the basketballs into a nearby door marked "showers."

There, I removed my shirt to behold the miracle of a brand-new life.

OOZY MUCUS

EYE-STALKS WITH UN-DEVELOPED EYES

HORRIBLE GURGLING LIKE DROWNING RAT

The shower room was a mess, dirty towels everywhere, and no other doors or windows.

I peeled the Slug off my skin and tried to clean it in the sink with some hand soap, but it started contorting and making unhappy noises. It seemed to have a sensitivity to chemicals of any kind, even soap.

"There, there," I said, trying to calm it down, wiping it with a towel and cuddling it. It relaxed and burrowed its "face" into my armpit.

I wondered if maybe it was hungry. I tried giving it a piece of Juicy Fruit gum, which it seemed to like. I guess Slugs are attracted to fruit. But I was pretty sure the gum didn't have any real fruit in it. I chewed a piece myself and blew a bubble, which popped all over my face. I was terrible at bubbles.

Its eyeless eye-stalks patted the gum stuck around my mouth, then continued to probe around my neck and face, like it was trying to get a read on what I looked like. I stared at the mushy pulsating gastropod, all gooey and full of promise. Slugs were still the grossest and most repulsive things ever. But if I looked at the little thing just right, and sort of squinted, I couldn't deny there was just a tiny bit of cute.

I found some old watermelon rinds in the trash and it slurped on those for a bit, but it really seemed like it just wanted to be held. I rocked it and hummed it a song. I guess Miss Chips inspired me, and I hummed "Ooo-la-la fromage," a catchy advertising jingle I'd once heard for cream cheese. The baby Slug seemed to like it.

"I will call you Cream Cheese," I said.

With Cream Cheese squished against my body, I felt a momentary peacefulness. To fill up the space, I started talking.

I starting telling it about my action figure collection. But I couldn't keep my mind off what I was really thinking about. So I spoke about how they kept putting me in charge of things. And about how I kept telling them I didn't want to do it, because weirdness was turning me into a ticking time bomb. But that I knew this excuse was ridiculous. The truth, I told Cream Cheese, was that I wasn't worried about the danger of weirdness. I was worried about myself. The last time there was a crisis, everything came within a mucus drop of getting destroyed by giant worms. Now things were heating up with the Slugs, and the Moles were trying to push me into leading them again. What if this time I blew it entirely? I couldn't handle it. I was too scared.

I sighed and squeezed the baby Slug. It felt good to open up to somebody. Even if it was a gelatinous blob who couldn't possibly understand a word I was saying.

Speaking of saying, I was suddenly aware that the sound of Miss Chips's log-sawing had been replaced by voices. I went to put the Slug down to go have a peek, but it started making noises again and tried to wrap itself around me, and I realized it didn't want me to leave it alone.

I picked it up and said "Shhh," and told it that I was going to teach it its first valuable skill for life in this world: spying. I put my shirt back on and carried it stealthily to the door. Even though its little eye-stalks were still unopened and blind, it poked them super quietly around the door frame. It had taken to spying like a pro. I was so proud.

The voices belonged to the dance committee. The Binkettes and Marco were complaining animatedly about having to come in tomorrow before the dance to clean up the colossal decorating disaster I'd caused. Although you could tell they were only acting like they were upset. Any inconvenience they felt about coming in on a Saturday was offset by their clear enjoyment of how much trouble I was in.

Miss Chips stood projecting ire in all directions. I guess her imaginary trip to the French countryside was over. "Fix. Tomorrow noon. Don't be late," was all she said before turning and slumping out the door.

The committee members were already in great moods when they were given the bonus gift of a very hyped-up Pennyworth. He charged into the gym demanding to know if anyone had seen me, as he was sure he'd spotted me running into the building and suspected that I'd stolen his greatest scientific discovery of the century.

This provoked a round of mocking from Marco and the Binkettes about his ridiculous "egg." But Becky, being in a triumphant mood, humored him, and said that if this was indeed a huge discovery, she might go so far as to be impressed. But what she was more likely expecting was that Pennyworth was full of hot air and would very soon be popping, like a balloon, filled with pig barf, sitting in a dumpster. These last visual add-ons had been provided by Marco and the Binkettes, and everyone laughed even though they really stretched the logic of the metaphor.

At that moment the science teacher came in and told Pennyworth that he'd had enough of whatever stunt Pennyworth was trying to pull and was leaving. Pennyworth tried to get him to wait because they were sure to find his discovery soon, and just look at the pieces of egg they'd found in the hallway. And when the science guy didn't seem impressed with that, Pennyworth tried threatening him that once he'd achieved fame and fortune he'd make the teacher pay copiously for his narrow-mindedness in the presence of greatness. And when that didn't work, he tried the only tactic he had left.

The science teacher departed.

And the Binkettes all made popping sounds, and Marco, using his theater training, did a pretty good rendition of a pig barfing.

Pennyworth lost it. He called everyone a bunch of four-syllable names and vowed that the science teacher and Becky and the rest of "you pathetic wretches" would soon be eating their words and praising Pennyworth's discovery as the most copiously important thing ever. Then, realizing he'd included Becky in this fire-bombing, he tried to pull a quick edit.

"Except you, Becky. You're still smart and cool and not a wretch at all."

"Pop," said Becky.

For someone who'd just become a megalomaniac recently, Pennyworth had got up to speed quick. His fists shook and he got all red and veins started popping out in his forehead. He vowed that he wasn't going to be humiliated like this, and swore he was going to get that scientist to return and validate his discovery, and we'd all be sorry when he did.

It was a pretty impressive pose. Some backlight came from somewhere. Too bad for him I was the only one to see it. The dance committee had already left, chuckling gleefully.

But for all his amazing pose-work, I wondered what he was doing swearing he'd have his discovery validated, since I had his little discovery tucked safely under my arm, the two of us as quiet as super-spy ninjas on a windless night. That is, until the Slug started nuzzling up against my face.

Pennyworth's head spun our way, and I ducked back into the shower room.

Had Cream Cheese really said "Da da"? I must have been hearing things.

"Da da! Da da! Da da!" it gurgled.

"Shhh!" I said, looking around the shower room. No windows, no other doors. We were trapped! What were we going to do?

I heard the patter of tiny feet rushing nearer, and the slam of a tiny foot kicking open the door, and the small squeal of pain from his foot being hurt on the door. But as for the look of disappointment on his face, I could only imagine it, as he found the room empty but for a pile of dirty towels in the corner.

10

MOLE LEVEL, THIS IS IT, NEVER AGAIN, I MEAN IT!

"**G**reat job, Oog!" I said as we hustled through the freshly dug tunnel.

Just as I was backing away from the door in anticipation of Pennyworth bursting into the shower room, a pair of muddy Mole hands tore through the floor beneath me and the baby Slug and pulled us under, before pulling a pile of towels back over the hole to hide our escape.

"It no biggie," said Oog, leading me quickly through the tunnel he had freshly dug. We were heading back to the Mole realm at top speed. I didn't know what a slime parsec of time was, but

I had to be running out of them by now. "Oog glad he able get you out of there. That other kid have look in eye like he about to chew rocks."

RUNNING AGAIN

MUDDY SHOES AGAIN

"Wait, how did you know I was in there?" I asked.

"Uhhhh . . . Oog happening by," said Oog.

I gave him a look, and Oog admitted he'd been following me again, even though I'd ordered him not to. He said he was in my backyard when I was confronted by Slugs, and had been watching me through a window on the far side of the gym.

"King so funny. Hide in big pile of balls," he snickered.

"So you were in my backyard when those Bull Slugs surrounded me?" I said. "They almost flattened me like a pancake!"

"Nah, Oog move faster than Slugs if they try pancake," said Oog.

"And that *was* you who put the pothole in front of the bus too, wasn't it? I keep ordering you not to follow me in the Up-world, but you keep disobeying!"

"It true," Oog said smiling. "But Oog not disobey! Because Oog not following King as Royal Guard. Oog following King as *friend*."

It was a nice feeling to have a friend who cared about you so much.

Or at least cared about you if you were King. But what if I wasn't King?

"Oog," I said, "why are you my friend?"

"Why friend?" said Oog. "Because King good at jokes, good with using brain . . . good at being King."

"So . . . you're my friend because I'm King?"

"Huh?" said Oog. "What King mean?"

But we'd reached the Moles' Big Cavern.

"Again, Quits-a-Lot? Seriously?" said the Round Mole.

"I've got no time for you, Round Mole," I said, pushing past him. Yes, I was back in the Mole realm again, but my plan was to make one quick exchange, and then that was it! Never again! This time I meant it!

"Let me guess," said the Round Mole, "this is the last time! Never again! This time you mean it!"

I ignored him and spoke to Lindoog. "Any word about Magda?"

Lindoog said Ploogoo and Boogo had escorted Magda down to the Slug level and they hadn't heard anything more. I told them about Magda's walkie-talkie scream. "It's going to be okay. I've got the thing that'll calm them down right here," I said, patting my tummy.

"King bring them fanny pack as gift?" said Oog.

I lifted my shirt to reveal the baby Slug squished against my stomach, causing all the Moles to reel back.

"Yuck!" said the Round Mole. "It looks like a wet sock filled with pudding!"

"Awwww," said Lindoog, caressing the little Slug's back. "Look how little she is."

"She?" I said.

"It's a girl Slug," said Lindoog. "You can tell by the mucus ganglia and salivary sacks."

Of course. How could I have missed those? My sweet little Cream Cheese was a baby girl. The cutest baby Slug girl anyone had ever seen.

At that moment one of the eye-stalks shuddered and an eye opened.

"Oog!" I said. "Grab my backpack! We have to get this baby back where she belongs! Lead us to Magda!"

"Bring Ploogoo back to me safe!" Lindoog called as we headed off.

"And bring me a T-shirt next time you come from the Up-world," called Round Mole.

At the edge of the hole leading to the Slug level, Oog tried to put the Mole crown on my head, but I told him my neck couldn't handle it. We dropped through to the level below and landed in slime, causing us to immediately fall down. I coaxed Cream Cheese from my stomach to my back, and we started pulling ourselves forward like a couple of seals.

We were making terrible progress when we ran into a Slug wearing a sash.

"Well, if it isn't little fuzzy-head, the Mole King," said Ambassador Sputz.

BEEEELCH!

(AUDIO EQUIVALENT OF A SLAP IN THE FACE)

"Greetings, Ambassador," I said. "What are you doing in this tunnel?"

"Taking a break from listening to that blowhard Gurge spout off. Thanks a bunch for telling the Bull Slugs about us. Things have been a real treat since they oozed into town."

"Sorry about that," I said.

"They've all got their keels in a knot about that deal we had with Croogy. It was you who told them about that as well, wasn't it?"

"Sorry about that too."

"King learn lesson about TMI," said Oog in my defense. "He not do it more."

"Before these guys came along, we were just called 'Slugs,'" said Sputz. "Then they identified themselves as 'Bull Slugs.' So now we're 'Common Slugs.' Not the catchiest name, is it?"

"I've got something for them that might help. Do you think you could give us a hand getting to them?"

Sputz gave me a "So now you want a favor?" sigh, then elongated appendages from his sides and started dragging us along the slippery ground back the way he'd come. I felt Cream Cheese oozing up my back and peeking out the neck of my shirt. She started making little noises that could have been "wheeeee"s. I guess this was like a wagon ride for her. Another landmark moment in a child's youth.

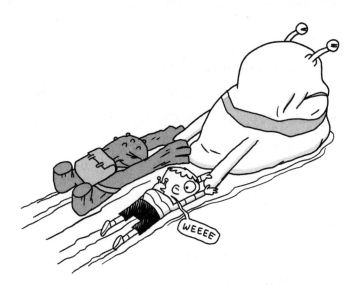

WEEEE

As Sputz pulled us along, Oog told me what a great job I'd done getting Ploogoo and Lindoog together. Thrusting them into a tricky situation in the Up-world had made them all "shmoopy shmoopy"!

"Going through an ordeal tends to bring people closer," said Sputz.

"So Ploogoo's more confident now?" I asked hopefully.

"Nope," said Oog. "Now he worried all the time about Lindoog. Confidence worse than ever."

We arrived at the Slugs' Big Cavern. It was the same as the Moles' Big Cavern, except with more goo. Also, instead of Moles it was filled with Slugs. Common Slugs on one side, and Bull Slugs on the other surrounding Ambassador Gurge. Another major difference was there was a Slug about three times as big as the others wearing a crown. And another difference was there was a Slug about five times as big as the others on the other side, also wearing a crown. It really wasn't much like the Moles' Big Cavern at all, come to think of it.

Sputz dragged us near the three-times-bigger King and introduced me. "This bag of ooze is King Hurrk, the King of the Common Slugs. Hurrk, say hi to the King of the Moles."

King Hurrk smiled goofily and took my hand from where it lay beside my body and shook it. "Charmed," he said, in a voice that sounded like a giant wet pillowcase filled with pudding. Which is sort of what he looked like too.

"Your names all really do sound like bodily function sounds," I said while Hurrk pumped my arm up and down.

"I dunno what yer talking about," said Sputz. "That Bull Slug monstrosity over there is King Burf."

The Bull Slug King was truly heart-stopping. If King Hurrk looked like a giant pillowcase filled with pudding, Burf looked like a whole bed filled with pudding. A pudding bed, with the ability to emit the most thunderous belches.

"Cutting it close, Mole King. Only three slime parsecs to spare," said Gurge. "I hope it wasn't too difficult for you sliding down the tunnel from your house after we slimed it."

"I didn't have to take that slime tunnel," I said. "My Royal Guardsman Oog brought me through the new tunnel he just dug that leads directly to my school."

Oog and Sputz gave me "TMI" expressions.

"Look," I said, "I'd rather be getting a tonsillectomy than be here right now, but like it or not I'm Mole King for at least the next three minutes. And as Mole King, I demand to see the Human Slug Ambassador and her guards so we can do this exchange and I can get out of here and never come back again! So what do you say? Are we doing this, or what?"

And that's when several Bull Slugs parted and I got to see this:

Magda, Ploogoo, and Boogo, suspended like raspberries in a Jell-O mold.

Even though I was pretty sure they couldn't hear me, I decided to yell "I told you so!" anyway. "I told you so"s feel so good to say you never want to miss an opportunity, whether someone can hear you or not. "Get them out of there!" I yelled.

"Where's the egg?" said Gurge.

Oog dug a spot in the slime so I could stand up. "I'm afraid it's not an egg anymore," I said, pulling the baby Slug off my back. Strands of gloop dangled between our torsos as I held her forth.

Immediately the Bull Slugs and Common Slugs banded together in a chorus of "ooh"s and "aww"s, fawning over sweet little Cream Cheese.

"Look, she already got her eyes," cooed Gurge.

"They just popped open an hour ago," I said.

Gurge took her from me, and I heard her say "Da da" again. "Heh heh," I snickered sheepishly, "she thinks I'm her daddy."

"She didn't say 'Da da,'" said Gurge. "She said 'ra ra,' like she's cheering, because she's so happy to be away from repulsively dry human skin."

"Take care of her," I said. "She likes watermelon rinds. And French songs. And she's really good at spying. And is a good listener. And likes riding on your back while nuzzling your ear. I named her Cream Cheese."

"Cream Cheese?" said Gurtz. "We'll give her a good Slug name, like Blorp or Splatz or Goosh."

The Bull Slugs burped in assent, then pulled Magda and Ploogoo and Boogo out of the globule. I knew from earlier that the goo was resistant to water, so I pulled some dry towels from my backpack and started wiping Magda off. This wiping goo off others was getting to be a habit.

I had a strange feeling I couldn't put my finger on. It was sort of like that time I lost an action figure down a toilet, and a plumber came and unclogged it, and then handed me back the figure. I was relieved my figure hadn't been lost down the drain. I guess it was a similar feeling I was having now about Magda, a sort of happiness to see her. I wondered if she was feeling anything similar about seeing me.

"I can't believe you knew about the Slug egg and didn't do anything about it!" she yelled. "You're so busy trying to sell your house, you don't care who gets hurt in the process!"

She was right. I felt terrible about it, and I couldn't really defend myself. But I still tried.

"Maybe you're the one who's selfish! I loan you my walkie-talkie, and now it's covered in slime!"

"There's people counting on you," she said, looking me right in the eyes, "but you're neglecting everyone, and blaming it on your ridiculous theory about weirdness destroying everything!"

"It's not just the weirdness . . . ," I mumbled. "There's another reason too . . ."

"Ugh, the blowhard is spouting again," said Sputz, and we turned toward Gurge. He was making a speech that seemed designed to rile up the Slugs, telling them that they've been getting kicked around like footballs filled with pudding ("pudding" was a go-to descriptor with these guys) by the upper levels for too long, and that they were once again being shortchanged on the deal that the Moles' former advisor Croogy had made on the Moles' behalf.

"All Croogy wanted to do was start a fight," I said. "Just ask him yourself."

"Oh, we would," said Gurge. "But apparently your former advisor has escaped and disappeared deeper into the earth."

"Well, this is all your guys' business to figure out," I said. "I just came to save Magda and give you the egg, and now, once and for all, *I quit being King!*"

Everybody started talking at once.

The Moles said I couldn't quit now in the middle of this sensitive crisis. Magda said she didn't need saving from a selfish jerk like me. And Gurge said he thought it was pretty convenient that as soon as I found out my girlfriend was in trouble I was suddenly able to produce the stolen egg, and that he suspected it was me who stole it in the first place.

"She's not my girlfriend!" I said. "And it wasn't me who stole the egg! It was this guy Pennyworth! He took the egg and stashed it at the school!"

"The place where the tunnel you just told us about leads to?" said Gurge.

Oog and Sputz and several others groaned. "Dude, you have really got to cork that mouthhole," said Sputz.

I said they didn't need to worry about my mouth anymore, because I was heading back to the Up-world where I belonged, and nothing, but nothing, was going to stop me.

Ahhh . . . , I thought. *So that's how Pennyworth was planning to prove his discovery to everybody.* I should have realized how far a snapped forehead vein would push someone.

The Slugs wasted no time in freaking out. There was a bunch of arguing about why the eggs hadn't been properly guarded, but my guess was they were guarding the entrance and didn't know about the little side-hole that Oog had made.

Gurge accused me of wanting to get out of there in such a hurry because I was behind this latest egg theft. I was going to say I already told them it was that Pennyworth guy, but I wondered if that was TMI again, so I tried to change it and say it was this guy named Bob. But that didn't seem to work.

"We'll get the eggs back! Won't we, Underbelly?" said Magda.

"No!" I cried. "I can't be involved! Weirdness vortex! Too dangerous!"

"We know where this Pennyworth person is!" said Gurge. "We'll get the eggs back ourselves! And we'll slime anyone who gets in our way!"

"Sheesh, Gurtz, it's always slime slime slime with you!" said Ambassador Sputz. "Don't be fooled by fuzzy-head here. The humans aren't all mealy-mouthed, lily-livered nose-wipes like he is."

I cleared my throat as the Bull Slugs looked at me, and told them Sputz was right, it was dangerous for them in the Up-world. The humans were indeed not all nose-wipes. Plus there were a lot more of them than they thought.

"How many?" Gurge asked.

"As many as the stars," I said.

"What are stars?" said another Bull Slug.

"Well, if there are so many humans," said Gurge, "I suppose we better take *all* the Slugs with us. The Bull Slug King challenges the Common Slug King to a *Great Slugging!*"

There was a huge sloshy rabble from the twin Slug assemblies. Whether the Common Slugs were up for it or not, a Great Slugging challenge cannot be refused.

Common Slug King Hurrk let out a huge battle-belch and moved his gelatinous bulk forward. He "ran" around the room in a long, slow circle, bellowing and taunting the much larger Bull Slug King, sticking out his tongue and making chicken sounds.

It was over in about five seconds.

King Burf let out an enormous victory belch. If whale calls were the loudest sound under the water, Slug burps were the loudest sound under the land. Not quite as beautiful as whale music, however.

11

THE SLUGS RISE

Ambassador Gurge declared that, by Slug law, the Slug tribes were now combined, and he was going to lead them up through the tunnel that led to the human school to retrieve their stolen eggs and slime everything in their wake. The Moles protested that this proposed path would leave the Mole level drenched with ooze, but Gurge said time was of the essence and they couldn't help it if the Mole level got slimed. I thought the Slugs were being pretty passive-aggressive.

I also thought they were being pretty aggressive-aggressive. They all grabbed spears and started shaking them. Ploogoo and Boogo seal-flippered toward the exit to get ahead of the Slugs so they could warn the Moles of the impending stampede. I took my backpack from Oog and tried to give the Mole crown to Ploogoo as he passed by, but he was preoccupied, probably thinking about Lindoog.

Oog took a few seal-flippers toward the exit, then flippered around and looked at me.

"Go help the Moles," I said. "You don't need to follow me. I'm not your King anymore."

He smiled. "You so funny . . . Underbelly," he said, then pushed himself off across the slime rocks to get ahead of the Slugs, leaving me holding the crown.

"We've got to warn anyone who's at the school!" said Magda, but I didn't move. "You can't be serious, Underbelly. You're really going to let everyone fend for themselves and not try to help just because you're worried about weirdness?"

"There's another reason—"

"Oh, right, your 'other reason.' What's this big 'other reason' you keep talking about?"

"Um, well, the other reason is . . . it's just that . . ."

"Yes??" said Magda.

"I've just had it with all these ground-in mud stains."

Magda did that thing where she squished her ping-pong eyes flat. Then she stormed off. As much as one can storm pulling themselves over slime-rocks on their belly. I yelled after her that it was too late, the Slugs had already started, the tunnel would be too slimed to get through. But she was in "ignore me" mode.

"You got a way with girls, Fuzzy Head," said Sputz. The cavern was emptying of Slugs. It was just him and me and the squished former Common Slug King, who Sputz was nursing.

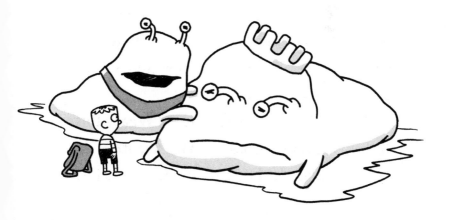

"I couldn't tell her the real other reason I can't be King anymore," I said.

"Because you're scared," said Sputz.

"How did you know?" I said.

"Slugs have a sixth sense for sensing fear."

"Really?"

"Of course not!" said Sputz. "It's just totally obvious. You're practically wetting yer pants off. Well, big whoop. Everybody's scared sometimes. You just gotta deal with it. Look at Hurrk here." He indicated the flattened former King lying before us. "Dancing around in front of the biggest Slug ever to ooze the Earth, pretending he was all brave. Although maybe taunting him wasn't such a good idea in hindsight."

"Is he going to be all right?" I asked.

"I dunno. How you doin', Hurrk, ya old bag of pudding?"

"It only hurts when I ooze," said Hurrk, and they laughed, until Hurrk coughed. Sputz held his head and poured some algae water into his mouth.

"Ol' Hurrk here and I go way back," said

Sputz. "When we were young I used to pound his back when he accidentally ate rocks. And he stood up for me when I shot my mouth off too much. He was never the sharpest root under the tree, but we always had each other's backs. That's what friends do. Stand by each other when they need you."

One of his eye-stalks swiveled toward me.

"I sorta thought that would be your eureka moment and you'd rush off to help your friends," he said.

"Yeah, I know, I'm getting there," I said. "It's just that last time I tried being King I almost destroyed everything. I'm still traumatized."

Former King Hurrk rolled his body so he could see me better, and said, "One surefire way of making things worse . . . is not taking any action at all."

I nodded at this wisdom.

"I dunno if *that's* true," said Sputz. "You can totally make things worse by doing things."

"Naw," said Hurrk, "doing something is always going to be more help than doing nothing!"

"You're nuts! If you blow it, you can screw things up even further!"

"We're defined by our actions, not our inactions!"

"You can always make things worse!"

They continued bickering like a couple of characters in one of those movies where you're supposed to understand that they actually love each other underneath. I pulled out my walkie-talkie. "Eagle to Squirrel, come in, Squirrel."

"You gotta be kidding! I'm Eagle!" said Magda.

"Forget about that for now," I said. "The real 'other reason' I didn't want to be King is . . ."

"You're too scared? Yeah, I know. I've got a 'sixth sense' about that too. Plus I'm only twenty feet away. You don't move very fast dragging yourself over Slug ooze."

"I just don't think I'm a very good choice to be King," I said.

"Well, you are inconsiderate, careless, erratic, uncoordinated, you give too much information, and your nose runs a lot," said Magda.

She paused. Unnecessarily long, it seemed
to me.

"But you're who the Moles want. And
your fear of weird things causing problems just
increases the chances that they *will* cause problems. So just try being a little brave. You've got
plenty of friends who are ready to help."

Sputz and Hurrk were still squabbling about
the pros and cons of doing something or doing
nothing, but I'd made up my mind. "I will take
action!" I yelled.

"Hooraaaaaay," said Magda sarcastically.

Every person in the lower realms was
currently in danger, because if a single Slug

Person got seen by a single human, the humans would turn this whole area into an excavation pit a mile deep. Even if the Slugs could be convinced to get out of the school before anyone saw them, they'd still leave an unexplainable amount of ooze all over the place. The same ooze they'd have already coated the tunnel with, so thick that it could never be cleaned, leaving it impassable to any non-Slugs.

We needed a plan. And I think I had one. I told Squirrel I had an assignment for her.

"I'm not being delivery person again!" said Magda.

"No," I said. "If I have to go all in on this, so do you. You're coming with me . . . deeper into the underground."

"Hey, if nothing else, going through an ordeal together will make you two closer," said Sputz.

12

ORDEAL

Magda and I dragged ourselves through the Slug tunnels where Oog had led me the last time I came down this way. The journey ahead was super serious. Yet still we couldn't help snickering a bit recalling Sputz and Hurrk bickering like a couple of three-year-olds.

"What if Sputz is right?" said Magda. "What if what we're about to go through is a huge ordeal? We may come out of here married!"

"It won't be that much of an ordeal!" I snapped back.

We got to the place where Oog had pried out a rock to gain access to the level below. We dropped into the lower tunnel, which was lined with huge stone blocks, and started making our way along it.

"Whoa, cool! Everything is made of stone!" said Magda.

"What did you think everything was going to be made of in the realm of the Stone Goons? Popsicle sticks?"

Her eyes shone in the dark. Even her marshmallow-white skin shone a little. With her pitch-black clothes and hair, she looked like a floating face. I was immediately sorry that I mentioned it.

"Booooooooooo . . . ," she said, pretending to be a ghost.

Magda questioned how heading down to deeper levels was going to help keep the Slugs from being discovered by humans. I told her not to worry, that I had "connections." And besides, the only way we could make things worse was by not taking any action at all.

"No, Sputz was right," said Magda. "You can totally make things worse by doing things."

"No way! Not doing anything is worse!" I said.

"If you screw up it can mess things up more!"

"We're defined by our actions, not our inactions—!"

"Who dares disturb the Stone Goons?" said a wall, in a familiar voice that sounded like gravel being poured. Just like last time, I didn't realize the walls had stopped being walls and started being Stone Goons until one of them spoke.

I pulled out my crown and put it on, and told Magda to let me handle this.

"It is I, Doug Underbelly, King of the Mole People!" I said.

STONE-FACED
REACTIONS
(I MEAN MORE
THAN NORMAL)

"Doug Underbelly," I repeated. "You know. I came through here with a Mole last month. You followed us through the Mushroom realm, brought a few Mushroom People with you to the Big Hole. It was clogged with a mountain of Up-world stuff. A worm the size of a steamship popped out at the end. None of this ringing a bell?"

The Goons began to explain that Stone Goon memory worked differently than ours. Transient happenings didn't make impressions in the same way. Where our memory moved like ripples on water, theirs moved like layers deep within rocks where movement was only detectible over vast periods of time.

"Oh, hi, Magda," one of the Goons said. "How are you?"

Sigh. So they remembered her, but not me. What was the use of being King if you didn't even command attention? I took off my neck-crunching crown.

"Wait, I am aware of this human," said one of the Goons, pointing at me. That was more like it. "He choked me with something called 'eel mac 'n' cheese.'"

"Yes, right, that was me," I sighed. "Any chance I can get that container back— Never mind. I've come because I need a favor."

This didn't exactly thrill them. I made a little speech about how friends helped friends, but that didn't help at all since they said friendship for Goons was like an animal skeleton trapped between two layers of rock, or something. Magda said not to worry, that other humans had just as much difficulty considering me a friend as they did, and they all laughed. It was the first time I'd heard Stone Goons laugh, and apparently it was something they only did every couple of years or so.

The Goon who had choked on the mac 'n' cheese introduced himself to Magda as Wall-Mall-A, and asked her what our favor was.

I told them about how angry Slug People had invaded the Up-world, and how if any humans saw them they'd summon these other humans called scientists, and they'd summon even more humans who'd come and unearth all the various creatures that live underground and probably do unkind things to them, and that the Slugs didn't realize how many humans there really are up there. The Goons asked how many.

"Uhh, like the number of rocks in your realm," I said.

"So, 97,556," said Wall-Mall-A.

They all grumbled at how daunting this number was, so I figured I didn't need to elaborate further. They put their stone heads close together and rumbled some more. Then they agreed that they would help me, as long as it didn't require any lifting.

"Uh, well, it does actually require some lifting," I said.

"We can't take any more lifting!" said another Goon. "Everything in our world is made of stone! Our backs are in constant pain!"

"Well then, great news!" I said. "What would you say if I told you I could eliminate all your back pain once and for all?"

"We would say: Is this offer contingent on us doing this lifting for you first?" said Wall-Mall-A.

"Yes," I said. "But keep in mind: human scientists."

They grumbled some more, and looked at Magda, who nodded to indicate that what I was telling them was valid. Then finally they gave their answer.

"We agree. We'll do your lifting. As long as whatever it is we're lifting isn't too unpleasant."

I was standing before a pack of Mushroom Folk in the next realm over from the Stone Goons. The large King Mushroom, identifiable by his tall size and spiky crown-like top, was yelling at me, aided by his subjects. I'd forgotten that Mushroom Folk felt threatened by other royalty and didn't take well to other kings in their midst. Did wearing this crown ever do anything positive for me?

"Please, Mushroom Folk," I said, removing my crown and stepping forward. "I mean you no harm!"

"Watch it!" came a little cry from beneath me.

"You almost stepped on my son again!" yelled the Mushroom King.

If the Stone Goons had a hard time remembering me, the Mushroom Folk seemed to remember every tiny transgression.

"Sorry, sorry!" I stammered. "Look, we need a favor."

"A favor? You mean like, can you bring us more ice cream?" said the King. "I sent word up to the Mole level that we demanded the Mole King bring more ice cream for the Mushroom Prince, and was told he wouldn't be caught dead in our realm unless all creation had frozen over! How dare you return to our kingdom without ice cream! My son is broken with sorrow!"

SOAK UP HIS BRAINS, DAD!

The cavern filled with Mushroom grunts as they tried to attack me, straining at the base of their stems as if refusing to acknowledge they were firmly stuck to the ground. Over their growls and insults, I tried to tell them about the dangerous events transpiring in the Up-world.

"The humans and the Slugs are going to hurt each other?" they said. "That's great! We hate all you other inferior creatures! Especially Slugs! The way their bodies squish and squirm, everything covered in ooze. Revolting!"

"You say you hate the Slugs," I said. "But they do one thing I know you like. Make slime! You guys love to eat slime!"

The Mushrooms conceded that indeed, the Slugs did make delicious slime. But the Mushroom Folk didn't do inferior creatures any favors, unless it was the favor of putting them out of their misery, if we dared to lie down close to them for an extended period of time so they could slowly grow onto us and then out of our spleens and eye sockets, etc.

"What would you say if I told you I could

get you all the ice cream the Prince could eat? Flavors that make eel ice cream taste like . . . something gross that lives in the bottom of a swamp."

"We do really like ice cream—that is, my little sprout really likes ice cream," said the King. "But we hate all of you more!"

"Yes," said the King's little sprout, "but let's not be too hasty about the ice cream . . ."

"Wait till you try Rocky Road. You'll flip your tops," said Magda.

And the cavern filled with Mushroom screams. "Ghost! Ghost!" they yelled, seeing Magda's accidental illusion of a floating face.

"That's right, I'm a ghost!" said Magda, picking up on their error. "Boooooooooooooo!"

"Haunt us no further, spirit!" they cried.

"I've come with a message from the ethereal wooooooorld," she said in a ghost voice. "But this message is only for the group of creatures who can prove themselves woooooooorthy."

"How, O spirit? How?" they cried.

"By proving they are the creatures who can eat the most sliiiiime!"

The Mushrooms' bravado began to overcome their fears and they started bragging about how they could eat more slime than all other creatures combined. Ghost Magda prodded them by saying that humans were pretty amazing slime-eaters too, and the Mushrooms swore they'd eat ten times the slime that pathetic humans could and ten times more again, just let them at it. And they started making grunting sounds and pulling at where their bodies met the ground. Ghost Magda pointed to me and said she'd appointed this nose-wipe human to be their earthly guide.

I called in the Stone Goons.

"This is what you want us to carry?" moaned Wall-Mall-A.

"Remember, I've got a back pain cure that'll have you sleeping at night like babies," I said.

"Stone Goons don't sleep," said one Goon.

"And Stone Goons are never babies," said another. "We reproduce by chipping pieces off our backsides and—"

"Okay, okay! We don't need the Stone Goon birds-and-the-bees talk!" I said.

I instructed the Goons to pick up the Mushrooms. The Mushrooms squawked and threatened to ravage things and destroy things and burst through things, but they didn't waste a lot of energy on it. They were saving themselves for the slime.

We started back to the Up-world. I was filled with dread. Magda took note of my expression.

"You're doing goooooood," she said.

"You can drop the ghost act," I said. "And I'm doing terrible! The only reason this is working out is that you keep saving the day."

"Having the right people at your side to help is still a win, Underbelly."

"What an ordeal," I said with a sigh.

"Fall in love with meeeeee!" spooked Magda.

13

SCHOOL

The Moles were all lying on their stomachs when we returned to the Big Cavern. I told them that, although I was indeed still technically their King as of that moment, now was not the time for praising and groveling. Then I realized they were all lying flat because they'd slipped on slime and couldn't get up.

The Slugs had slimed the Mole level bad on their way to the Up-world, and a lot of the Moles were having a pretty hard time. Ploogoo and Lindoog were spearheading the helping of smaller and older Moles, trying to get them out of the slime and cleaned off. Magda noted how well the two of them worked together.

They seemed even happier with each other than before. I guess with me around, there was never a shortage of ordeals.

The Moles and Goons would probably have bristled more at the unprecedented appearance of Goons in the Mole realm, but both were too occupied with their own situations at that moment. The Mushroom Folk bristled, but they were always bristling, so that was about as expected.

But wait. How did we all get from the Slug level to the Mole level with the Slug slime coating the tunnels? Great question, if you asked it.

When we reached the slime, Ghost Magda said "Booooooo," and told the Mushrooms that they could commence eating slime to show their worthiness to receive the ethereal message. They started grunting and trying to eat slime, even though there was no way they could reach it from the Goons' backs. Then I indicated to the Goons that they should point the ends of the Mushrooms to the slime and move them around, allowing the Mushrooms to suck up the slime like vacuum cleaners (or dust busters, if they were smaller ones).

It worked amazingly well, and slime began disappearing, revealing ground that could be stepped on without falling on your butt.

I told Ploogoo and Lindoog and the other Moles that they were doing a great job helping all the Moles in the Mole realm, and promised I'd be back to pitch in just as soon as I fixed everything with the Slugs and humans. I waved at Oog on the far side of the chamber, but he didn't wave back. Was he too busy to see me? Or was he just too busy for someone who quit being King?

I told the Goons to start Mushroom-vacuuming the tunnel that led to the school.

About an hour later, Magda and I poked our heads out of the hole beside the gym that Oog had first come out of, where he'd watched me through the window hiding in a bin of basketballs. The sun was up, which meant it was Saturday morning. The day of the dance.

We tried to look through the windows to see if we could see any Slugs. We couldn't. But that was because the windows were so thick with slime you couldn't see through them.

Before we did anything else, we needed to recover the missing eggs and get some supplies.

I handed Magda a list.

"You're not!" I assured her. "It's just really important that you be the one to pick up these supplies from the store and deliver them to me, since I have to check the science portable for the missing eggs. And also because I need you to pay for the stuff, since I'm broke."

She snatched the list with a growl.

I headed to the science portable to retrieve all the stolen Slug eggs. There was no doubt in my mind that someone as narrow-minded as Pennyworth would simply hide the eggs in the same place he'd hid them last time. But once I got there and found no eggs, some doubt started forming.

Magda and I rendezvoused at a school entrance, where she dumped a bag of store items at my feet.

"I swear this is the last time I'm doing this!" she said.

"Don't swear that you're doing anything for the last time," I warned, shoving the items into my backpack. "Take it from me."

The windows on the school doors were also coated in ooze, and the door made a loud SHLOOP! sound as I forced it open.

The hallway was so slimed from top to bottom it was barely recognizable. I could sort of make out the water fountain I'd been sprayed in the face with. And I thought that was the locker I'd once been locked inside of. But the place bore more of a resemblance to the inside of a worm than a school. Thankfully there were no Slugs in sight. And no humans either, which wasn't surprising since it was Saturday. But it wouldn't be long before the dance committee showed up to decorate the gym. We had to get this cleaned up pronto.

"It looks like the inside of a worm," said Magda.

"Hey, I thought the same thing!" I said. And we smiled at each other. "Let's get the vacuums."

The procession of Goons carrying Mushrooms snaked from the hole to the school doors, with Magda and me at its head, each clutching a midsize mushroom. We looked at each other with a "Let's do this" expression.

I stepped into the ooze and held tightly to the wall. Wall-Mall-A was behind me carrying the Mushroom King and his tiny sprout son. I motioned for them to follow, telling them to be sure to keep very, very quiet.

"*This* is the Up-world? What a dump!" yelled the Mushroom King. The Mushrooms entering on the backs of Goons jeeringly agreed. "The Up-world is disgusting!"

"Even the ghost looks lame up here," yelled the Mushroom Prince, giving Magda the up-and-down.

Magda shrugged. "This is just how I manifest up here. But I still have the power to haunt you! Boooooooooo!"

The Mushrooms got scared again and got to work on the slime, cleaning the walls and also the floors so we could walk on them.

"I guess you can get off my case about cleaning my room after seeing a swamp like this!" said the Mushroom Prince.

"You'll still clean your room!" said the Mushroom King.

I snickered.

"Quiet, you hairy, dry-skinned big nose!" said the Prince.

"Is that really necessary?" I said.

"I'm probably overcompensating, but look at me! I'm an inch-high fungus!" he squealed. "And where's my ice cream?"

As we made our way through the school, Magda and I checked each room for the Slug eggs. Pennyworth had to have the eggs somewhere on the school property if he was going to make good on his boast to have the science teacher and everyone eating their words and singing his praises. I don't know a lot about megalomaniacs, but they seem pretty driven when it comes to fulfilling their boasts.

The more rooms we ruled out, the more likely it was that Pennyworth had taken the eggs directly to the gym, which was doubtlessly the epicenter of the Slug invasion force. Which would mean that our goal to keep any humans from seeing any Slugs might already be shot. And the Slugs might already be in serious danger.

We started hearing a low, gravelly rumble. I didn't know what sort of thing the Slugs were doing that would cause such a sound. Then I realized it was coming from close by.

It was the Goons.

The Mushrooms were getting more bloated and heavy with all the slime they were consuming. "Our backs . . . ," groaned the Goons. "Too much lifting . . ."

I told the Goons not to fret, all their back-pain prayers were about to be answered. I reached into my backpack and pulled out some back-pain ointment. I squirted it onto Wall-Mall-A's back and began massaging it in. As much as you can massage something into rock.

"Burning . . . tingling . . . ," said Wall-Mall-A. Then he stretched himself up to his full height. "I feel fantastic!"

The other Goons quickly formed a line, and Magda and I applied the ointment.

SULLEN GOON **MASSAGE IN OINTMENT** **HAPPY GOON !**

The Goons were revitalized, and they started moving the Mushrooms up and down over the slime at twice the speed of before.

"Look at us go!" cackled the Mushroom King. "Humans could never come close to eating the amount of slime we can eat!"

"I dunno, you've never been to a street carnival," said Magda.

Magda went to check a supply closet, and told me to check the boys' bathroom.

"Why," I said, "too scared to go into the boys' room?"

"Of course not," she said. "Why would I be afraid to go in there?"

"Because it's the boys' room. You're afraid, just admit it."

"You gotta be kidding," she said, storming toward the door with the little pants-wearing silhouette on it. "It's just a stupid boys' bathroom! What on earth could be inside that I might possibly be afraid of?"

The Slug that came out seemed just as surprised as we were. He bobbled his spear and his newspaper, before finally dropping the paper and pointing his spear at us with both appendages. At the same time I was bobbling the tub of handsoap I'd pulled out of my backpack. I knew from my time with the baby Slug how much Slugs hated this stuff. I aimed it in front of the Slug and pumped the dispenser.

The Slug dropped his spear and slithered at top Slug speed toward the gym. I called after him to wait, but he was hysterical, racing down the hall at a good one or two miles per hour.

"See? We just went through adversity and don't feel any closer to each other at all," I said.

"Maybe that's something that only happens to Moles," said Magda.

Even at his slow pace, the Slug was eventually going to make it to the gym and blow the whistle on us, so we figured we'd better head there too.

I told the Goons and Mushrooms to keep cleaning every bit of slime they could find while we went on without them.

"No fair!" yelled the Mushroom Prince. "You said if I ate my slime there'd be ice cream!"

"Yes!" said the King. "You said we would have—that is, that my son would have ice cream!"

I reached into the backpack and pulled out several tubs of ice cream, and all the Mushrooms leaned in excitedly. There was a glorious selection of flavors far beyond the eel-flavored ice cream they'd tried. They were now spiraling into a universe of fudge, toffee, nuts, and cookie dough. Their fungal minds were being blown right through their lids.

"I'm the king of the world!!" yelled the Mushroom King's son, literally submersed in a half-melted carton of mint chocolate chip.

"Hmm," said the Mushroom King, licking his lips. "Not as good as the eel."

Score one for my dad.

Wall-Mall-A took the Mushroom King and vacuumed a path through the slime up to the gym door, where the out-of-breath hysterical Slug was just arriving. He swiveled an eye-stalk at us as we opened the door for him and waited as he slowly dragged himself through. We chatted while we were waiting.

"Sounds like they're doing a number on your dance decorations," said Magda.

"Maybe we should change the name to 'Slimetime in Paris,'" I said.

"Or 'the gym-nausium,'" said Magda.

The Slug had stopped in the doorway. "You guys are going to draw a lot of attention when you go in there. Everyone's going to look this way," he said.

"So?" I said.

"So I'm going to get in trouble if they see I lost my spear," he said.

"You won't get in trouble," I said.

"Would you mind if I went in after you? There's a better chance they won't notice then."

I sighed and said fine, and he started backing out. We returned to chatting.

"If Pennyworth ran into the Slugs in there," I said, "then once again everything has turned catastrophic, with me in charge, just like I was afraid of. Pennyworth could be on his way here right now with an army of scientists and an army of . . . army."

"Like usual, you're giving yourself too much credit, Underbelly," said Magda. "You're not responsible for everything that's happening."

I told her I was the one who told the Bull Slugs about the Common Slugs, and informed them about the deal Croogy made, and let them know there was a tunnel to the school.

"Okay, you might be responsible," said Magda.

"Yeah, you sound pretty responsible," agreed the Slug.

"Would you get out of the way already!" I said.

"But even if Pennyworth has seen the Slugs," said Magda, "all we gotta do is convince the Slugs to leave before Pennyworth returns with anyone else. Because nobody believes anything he says."

I hadn't thought of that. Megalomaniacs have a very hard time convincing people of things. As long as Pennyworth was the only human who'd had an encounter with the Slugs, things might just turn out to be okay.

The Slug finished backing up, and we went through the gym door.

Things were not going to be okay.

14

GYM-NAUSIUM

As someone who's always hated sports, I have no love for the gymnasium. But even I never wanted to see it in as sorry a state as this.

Ooze dripped from the walls. Bull Slugs and Common Slugs filled every corner. And just inside one of the free-throw lines, Miss Chips hung suspended, motionless like Magda had been, in a slime globule.

"Assembly of Slugs! Listen to me!" I called out. "You are all in grave danger!"

The Slugs laughed at the thought that *they* were the ones in danger—why should they fear any creatures that don't even know how to slime? The nearby Slugs lowered spears at me, and Ambassador Gurge slid forward.

"We want our eggs back!" he said. "And until we get them we're going to capture every human we find in retaliation! Guards! Add these two to the globule!"

"Wait!" I pulled the crown from my backpack and put it on. "I'm still King of the Mole People!"

"I thought you quit," said a number of Slugs.

"And as King, I declare diplomatic immunity!" I said.

There was a rumble through the Slugs. As a monarchy themselves, they respected the authority of crowns.

"You claimed the eggs would be here!" said Ambassador Gurge. "You lied!"

"I didn't lie! I'm sure the eggs are around here!" I said.

"Did you see this one human," said Magda, "veins sticking out of his forehead, says 'copious' a lot, really tiny feet?"

Gurge said this nonsensical description did not help lessen their suspicion that this "Pennyworth" person we kept talking about was made up to cover our own involvement in the egg stealing. If he really existed, then where was he?

It was a good question. In one way it was a

relief the Slugs hadn't seen him. But he'd vowed to prove himself to the science teacher in front of everyone right here in the gym. So where was he? Was it possible he didn't steal the eggs? There were a lot of eggs in that egg chamber. Was it possible they miscounted?

"We didn't miscount!" bellowed Gurge.

"Maybe you did!" I said, growing more confident in my theory.

"This is typical disrespect for Slugs and their offspring!" said Gurge.

"The Slugs are the ones disrespecting humans!" I said. "I'm starting to think humans have been wrongly accused! That we had nothing to do with any missing eggs at all! And you owe us an apology!"

Then we heard a noise coming from outside. Everybody in the gym went silent. It was the noise of the groundskeeper's new tractor. It grew louder as it approached the exterior of the gym, then shut off. Then came a series of clunks, the sounds of some items being loaded into something. Everyone passed glances to each other while we listened. Then there was a squeaking, like a wheel that needed oiling. It receded, then grew again as it echoed in the hallway outside the gym, growing louder, closer, until it reached the gym door. A tiny foot slammed into the door decisively, banging it open.

Gurge looked at me grimly.

"See? He exists," I said.

"Ohh," "Veiny forehead," "Tiny feet," mumbled the Slug throng.

The expression on Pennyworth's face went from cartoonishly extreme determination to cartoonishly extreme disbelief so fast it made his cheeks buckle.

He stood before a massive assembly of a new species of creature never before recorded in the science books.

For a moment, nobody moved.

Then the silence was broken by the sound of cracking eggs. Eggs that, in the face of a hundred full-grown adults, had become meaningless to Pennyworth. But not to the Slugs.

"Our eggs!" yelled the Slugs, grabbing the wheelbarrow from Pennyworth. He didn't even try to stop them.

"This is the greatest discovery of the century," he mumbled. "I'll be awarded the Nobel Prize. I'll be on the cover of *Time* magazine. I'll have my face chiseled onto the moon."

"Underbelly already discovered them, puny feet," said Magda.

"Nobody's going to listen to you anyway, Pennyworth! You've very unbelievable," I said.

"They will when the scientist confirms it!" said Pennyworth. "He's on his way back here right now!"

"There's no way you got that science teacher to agree to come back after your last humiliating fiasco," said Magda.

"Oh, you're copiously wrong," said Pennyworth.

WAVING WALLET. NOT SURE WHOSE. OH WAIT, MUST BE THE SCIENCE TEACHER'S.

Well, at least I was right about megalomaniacs' dedication to fulfilling their boasts. Pickpocketing is pretty low on a more sophisticated megalomaniac villain's crime list, but for a seventh grader it's some pretty diabolical stuff.

"Assembly of Slugs!" I yelled. "You must all flee back to your homes!"

"You creatures aren't going anywhere!" said Pennyworth, running for the door.

"Don't let that guy get away!" yelled Magda.

And suddenly the Slugs and us were united by a shared goal. We were allies.

Painfully slow allies.

Once you got the lead on a Slug, the race was pretty much done. Pennyworth disappeared out the door. And then we weren't allies again.

"You tried to convince us that you humans didn't take our eggs!" said Ambassador Gurge. "You were in on it the whole time, just as I suspected! Seize them!" Then, to a Slug standing near us, "You there! Where's your spear?"

"Uhh . . . ," said the Hysterical Slug.

A couple of spear-holding Slugs grabbed me.

"Take the eggs and get out while you can!" I yelled. "You have to listen to me!"

"We're tired of listening to what everyone says to us!" said Gurge. "'Gross,' 'slimy,' 'disgusting,' 'icky,' 'yucky'! We've been disrespected enough! If you don't respect us, then we don't respect you, or your stupid Mole crown!"

He knocked the crown off my head.

Then the Slugs grabbed Magda. And I lost my cool.

"Get your gooey appendages off her!" I ordered. "I command you!"

"Command?" scoffed Gurge. "Only the Slug King can make commands!"

"Then I challenge the Slug King to a *Great Slugging*!" I yelled.

"What?" yelled Magda, struggling against the Slugs that held her. "Underbelly, what are you doing? Look at the size of that King Slug!"

"I'm being brave like you said!"

"That's *too* brave!"

"*Why didn't you tell me there's such a thing as too brave?*" I screamed.

The words "Great Slugging" seemed to awaken the King Bull Slug from dozing, and he cast his eye-stalks about the room, looking for whoever was brainless enough to have said it. He found a room full of Slugs snickering and pointing appendages at me. Ambassador Gurge silenced the laughs, saying that all Great Slugging challenges had to be taken seriously. He snickered a little himself while saying this, but waved an appendage in the air and yelled, "Commence Slugging!"

The King Bull Slug oozed toward me, full of the confidence of a lawn mower about to take on a blade of grass. Drops of ooze fell off him that were bigger than me.

My first plan was to run. But I'd heard a line in a movie that running wasn't a plan, it's what you did when your plan failed. So I came up with another plan. I took out gum and started chewing.

"What are you doing now?" yelled Magda.

"I'm going to temporarily blind him by blowing a huge bubble and splatting him with it right in the eye-stalks!" I said.

"Is that bubble gum?"

"No!"

"How many pieces do you have?"

"One!"

"Aren't you terrible at blowing bubbles?"

"Maybe you could just be quiet and let me focus!"

I had to blow a bubble right this time, and it had to be a big one. I blew, and blew, and blew.

I did it! I'd blown a giant gum bubble!

The shadow of the King Slug fell over me as he leaned in, preparing to engulf me in his ooziness.

I tossed the gum bubble into the air and prepared to bat it toward his eye-stalk with my hand.

I ran.

The King Slug began "chasing" me around the room. He was so slow it wasn't much of a chase, but the other Slugs lined the edges of the room, preventing any escape, and began chanting, "Slugging, Slugging, Slugging."

"Underbelly! Take this!" yelled Magda, and tossed me the tub of hand soap. I squirted a soap-line on the floor in front of me.

The King Slug reeled back in disgust, then tried to go around it. I squirted another line.

I realized I could influence his direction in this way, at least till the soap ran out. But then what? How was I going to win a Great Slugging with the hugest Slug the world had ever known?

Magda was pointing wildly at the Eiffel Tower, still crushed into the ceiling and leaning at a precarious angle.

"Yeah, I know, I'm also in trouble for damaging the ceiling, thanks for bringing that up right now," I said, laying down another squirt. But she continued jabbing her finger at the tower, hanging there at such a sharp angle that it looked like it was going to topple over any minute, and then I finally understood what she was getting at.

"Ohhh . . . hide under the Eiffel Tower!" I said.

"No, doofus!" she yelled, and pointed at the Slug King and made a fist, and then made her other hand flat and had it sort of go "timberrrrr" onto the fist really hard.

I gave up trying to figure out what she was doing, because I suddenly got the idea that maybe I could get the Eiffel Tower to fall *on top* of the Slug King!

I squirted hand soap, creating a path to the tower. The King Slug hissed in disgust at the soap and pursued me down the path until he was directly under the tower. I tossed the empty soap tub aside and started kicking and pulling the tower, trying to get it to fall. But it was stuck fast.

The Slug moved in for the crush.

"It's not working, Underbelly! Run!" yelled Magda. Which was a great idea. But I didn't have anywhere to run to. So I started climbing the tower.

The gym filled with Slug gasps as I scrambled up, avoiding the King Slug's appendages as he tried to reach me through the bars. I made it to the top and started jumping up and down, getting the whole tower rocking.

The King Slug blinked as debris from the ceiling fell into his eye-stalks. Then a loud sound filled the room as the tower ripped free from the ceiling. It was the sound of me screaming.

"DOUG!!" yelled Magda.

15

SLUGGED

Nobody moved while the dust settled.

Then an appendage reached out from under the collapsed tower. In the appendage was a very large crown. The appendage stretched out and dropped the crown on top of me.

At first I thought the battle was still on, and this was the King Slug's retaliation. But then Gurge slithered forward and said, "Doug Underbelly, we crown you . . . King of the Slug People!"

A huge chorus of burps and cheers rang forth.

"Wait!" I sputtered, coughing out bits of ceiling shrapnel and trying to shove off the crown. The last thing I was after was *another* job as king! And it turned out the Slugs were anxious to get me out of office as well. The burps and cheers were immediately followed by a whole chorus of challenges to more Great Sluggings.

"I just want you to listen to me for one minute," I yelled, "and then you guys can make whoever you want your King!"

"Transfers of kingship can only happen through Great Sluggings," said Gurge. "And Great Slugging challenges cannot be refused."

"But I need to speak first! It's really important!"

"Form a line on the left! Who's the first challenger?" said Gurge.

There was a small, cute Slug burp. The Hysterical Slug pushed through the crowd. He was holding little Cream Cheese.

"Okay, I guess I could take her on in a Great Slugging," I said. "But then after that I really need you to listen to what I have to—"

"She's not challenging you," said the

Hysterical Slug. "She just really wants to see you."

And the Hysterical Slug put Cream Cheese into my arms, where she nuzzled and cooed and caressed my cheeks with her eye-stalks. I was so happy to see the little pudding pop.

"You're pretty good with kids, Underbelly," said Magda.

Gurge watched for a moment as if confused. "All right," he finally said. "Before you are crushed beneath an onslaught of Slugging, you may speak."

I told them again that they had to get out

of there, that humans were coming. The Slugs responded that with their combined tribes they would slime whatever number of humans that came. I got the impression they didn't fully realize how many humans there *actually* are. That maybe they thought this gym was just the human's "Big Cavern," and that the school was the entire Up-world.

"Don't be ridiculous," said Gurge. "Of course we know there's more to the Up-world than just this one building."

I apologized.

"How many more buildings are there? Ten? Twenty?"

"Uhh . . . more like millions of buildings. And then lots of space between the buildings. And then oceans of water around the spaces. And then above all that, more space. Once you start going up, you never really get to the top."

The Slugs murmur-burped at this information.

"But more importantly," I said, "we respect you, and your right to raise your children in peace."

The sounds of hatching filled the room. And everyone realized without saying it that the most important thing was getting these cute new babies somewhere safe.

"Everybody stay where you are!" yelled Pennyworth, reappearing in the doorway.

"You can't keep us here, little feet!" said Gurge. "The Slugs have decide to leave!"

"Not so fast!" said Pennyworth, which was accidentally a funny thing to say to Slugs. And he himself wasn't moving too fast either. He stepped forward with some difficulty, like he was weighed down. Some kind of white substance spilled from him in various places.

POWER POSE

SOME KIND OF WHITE SUBSTANCE

WHAT WAS IT?

"Salt!" bellowed Pennyworth.

Ah! He'd packed his clothes with cafeteria salt!

"That's right! Copious amounts of salt!" cackled Pennyworth. "It'll cause you Slugs to shrivel and die! And I've lined all the doors with it! You're trapped! And you can't touch me either because I also put salt in my clothes so that—"

Yeah, yeah, we got it, quit explaining everything, megalomaniac.

The Slugs recoiled in horror. They dropped their spears and "ran" (slowly moving forward) to the window that led to the tunnel outside. Pennyworth heaved a bag of salt at the floor near the window, and it exploded, sending Slugs "fleeing" (slowly turning and moving the other way). Everyone in the room was slithering and whimpering.

"The scientist is on his way!" declared Pennyworth. "He seemed very interested in getting his wallet back! There'll be no humiliation for me this time!"

"We gotta get everyone out of here!" Magda yelled to me.

I handed Cream Cheese to her. "Keep her from getting squished," I said. "I'll take care of Pennyworth."

I stepped forward. The Slugs may not have been able to touch Pennyworth in his salt suit. But I could. Salt couldn't hurt me.

"You've caused me copious amounts of trouble, Underbelly! But it's all over now! The scientist will be here any minute, and so will the dance committee! Then Becky will see how great I am! Where are they, anyway? It's ten past noon already."

At that moment, almost in unison, all the baby Slugs cracked through their shells.

I lunged at Pennyworth, and he hit me in the eyes with more salt. "AHHH!" I screamed again. Man, that stuff burned.

"Keep your eyes closed, Underbelly!" yelled Magda.

"I can't see! I need some water!"

"Did Underbelly say water?" said a familiar broken-Englished voice, and a stream of water hit me right in the face, cleaning the salt out of my eyes. I looked up and saw Oog sitting at the window, smiling at me, holding a hose.

"Oog!" I gagged. "Stop-*ghak*, pointing it-*ghak*, at my face-*ghak*!"

"Oops, sorry," said Oog.

He took the hose off me and pointed it at Pennyworth.

"You're still helping me? Even if I'm not your King?" I said.

"What, you think Oog got some kind of obsessive fascination with crowns? That silly. Of course, Oog heard King get new Slug crown . . . Whoa, look at it . . . so smooth and shiny . . ."

"Come on, cut it out!" I said.

"Oog just kidding!" he laughed. "Oog not love King because he King. Oog love King because he Underbelly. Of course Oog prefer call King 'King.' 'Underbelly' sort of roll off Oog's tongue funny . . ."

During all this Oog had been holding the

hose on Pennyworth, who was yelling about how the salt was dissolving and running into his nether regions, and some megalomaniac stuff like how he was going to get us for this.

Magda took the last item from my backpack. "Watermelon-flavored breath spray?" she said. "Why did you ask me to get this?"

"Because," I said. "Newborn Slugs go nuts for it."

Magda smiled and sprayed it all over Pennyworth.

The Slug babies didn't even have their eyes open yet, but they all shimmied and cooed at their first whiff of watermelon. It was a moment only the hardest of hearts could resist being warmed by.

Wall-Mall-A and the other Goons filed into the gym carrying Mushrooms that were groaning and bloated to the point of bursting. "We did it!" boasted the Mushroom King. "We cleaned the whole Up-world! It's still a pigsty, but at least we sucked up all the slime!"

"I can't wait to blow this dump, Pop," said the Mushroom Prince.

"Wait! Where's that ghost?" said the Mushroom King. "We proved ourselves to be the greatest slime-eaters ever! What is our ethereal message from the other side?"

"Uhh . . . the message is . . . ," said Magda, "that Mushrooms are the best!"

The Mushrooms paused. Then they all started shouting and woo-hooing in victory.

Pennyworth was going nuts—now there were even *more* types of unknown creatures? "Where's that scientist? And Becky! And the rest of that dim-witted dance committee?" he cried from beneath the swarm of newborn Slugs.

I didn't know the answer to those questions,

but I knew every minute counted and we had to get out of the school.

"We might have been a little hasty about taking over the Up-world," said Bull Slug Ambassador Gurge. "Some of you humans are actually pretty decent. Plus we forgot about salt."

I told Gurge that was great, and to tell everyone to grab the babies and get the former King out from under the tower and hurry through the window down the hole. He told *me* to tell them, since I was Slug King after all. We gave each other a little smile that said, *hey, you're all right, and I respect you.*

"We can take care of your Great Slugging challenges once we're back on our level," he said.

"Uhh . . . ," I said.

Pennyworth started yelling again once the Slugs peeled the Slug babies off him, so Oog held him in place with the hose while the procession started out the window.

The Goons and Mushrooms said they'd eaten the slime from the rest of the school, but the Mushrooms were too full now to do the whole gym. They cleaned up the floors as best they could after the departing Slugs, but the walls and windows and everything else were still covered in ooze.

I said I'd think of something. It was more important now for everyone to get back underground before anyone else saw them. The Slugs squeezed their huge King through the window (it was amazing how they could squish through spaces much smaller than themselves), as well as the last of the bloated Mushroom Folk, who couldn't wait to tell everyone how bad the humans were at eating slime and how overrated the Up-world was.

"Wait!" I screamed. "We still need to get my teacher out of the slime globule!"

I stood before Miss Chips. Of all the scary things I'd witnessed, she still took the cake. What if she was just biding her time in there, gearing up to laser-vision our heads and bury us in anthills?

"Come on, Underbelly," said Magda. "We can do this. Together. Just take a deep breath. Ready?"

We plunged our arms in and pulled.

We propped her back on her folding chair. Now that she was out of the globule her snoring could be heard loud and clear. Wall-Mall-A ran the Mushroom King over her to remove the excess gunk, and we leaned her little TV and garbage bag full of marshmallows against her. The Mushroom King took one of the marshmallows.

"I thought you were stuffed," I said to him.

"I'm going to explode if I eat this," he said. "Somebody stop me."

As Wall-Mall-A and the Mushroom King and Mushroom Prince were about to go through the window, I called after them, and they turned. I wanted to thank them for breaking my weirdness curse, for working together for the good of all our species, and for believing in me enough to follow me to this strange, forbidden land.

But there wasn't time for that at that moment, and I was also really bad at speeches. So I just let the moment linger, hoping a meaningful gaze between us would convey my sentiments better than words. "Here," I said, tossing Wall-Mall-A the tube of back ointment.

Oog picked it up and handed it to the Goon, and they disappeared through the window.

"See you later, Underbelly?" said Oog from the ledge.

"Definitely," I said.

"No! You can't go!" yelled Pennyworth, finally freed from Oog's hose. "Everyone's supposed to be here by now! Where *are* they? *I won't be humiliated again!*" He stood up, and his clothes fell off. Chewed apart by baby Slugs.

Oog pulled the hose through the window and shut it behind him. A second later the gym doors burst open, and in walked the dance committee.

They stopped, aghast at the condition of the gym. The torn ceiling, the mangled Eiffel Tower, and the thick layer of slime on the walls. And Pennyworth, standing soaked in his underwear.

"NOOOOOOOOOOOOOOOOOOO!" yelled Pennyworth, falling to his knees as megalomaniacs do when their schemes have been crushed.

This caused Miss Chips to finally wake up, and she added a growl to Pennyworth's scream. I guess she'd slept through the whole thing start to finish, as she made no mention of globule imprisonment or subterranean creatures. The only thing on her mind was that the dance space she was supposed to be supervising the decorating of was in a state not fit for habitation by human or beast.

"What are you monsters doing?" she yelled. "What happened to the Eiffel Tower? What's with all this slime? How is this supposed to be Springtime in Paris?!"

"Springtime in Paris?" I said. "I thought it was 'Slimetime in Paris.'"

The committee erupted. How idiotic was I to misunderstand the name of the dance theme? There was no such thing as "Slimetime in Paris."

Only a weirdo like me would somehow mistake "spring" for "slime."

Miss Chips quivered for a bit, and her head sunk so low between her shoulders that I thought it was going to disappear inside her body like a turtle. Or a Whac-A-Mole.

That is, until one of the Binkettes suggested that there was no way they were going to get this place ready in time for that evening, so there was no choice but to postpone the dance. Then Miss Chips's head popped back up to full neck-height.

"No way! I'm not going through all this again!" she said. "We're doing this dance tonight!"

Becky was happy—her plan had gone perfectly. Once again I'd been brought in to be in charge of something because I could be counted on to fail, and once again I hadn't disappointed. She announced that she would save the day by taking back the job as head of the committee. Everyone cheered.

I was kicked off the dance committee

entirely. Perfect. Now just two more crowns to get rid of.

Pennyworth said everything in screams now. He screamed that all the slime wasn't put there by me, but by giant slugs. Everyone laughed.

Then he screamed at the science teacher who finally showed up looking for his wallet. He screamed that the place had been full of multiple species of never-before-seen creatures. Slug People! Mushroom People! Even a Mole Man! He screamed at him and Becky and everyone for being so late!

They said they weren't late, they'd all arrived at noon. But someone had put up a brick wall in front of the doors and they couldn't get inside. They'd walked around the whole school, but brick walls blocked every door. The walls were so odd, they almost looked like primitive statues with brick arms and legs. Then suddenly a few minutes ago they were gone. It was the weirdest thing.

"Those were guys made of stone!" screamed Pennyworth.

The science teacher told Pennyworth that

scientists are about truth and don't pick pockets and don't make up stories and tend to wear pants, and that Pennyworth was a disgrace.

Pennyworth fell to his knees and yelled "Noooooooooo!" again. I'm not sure if he forget that he'd already done that, or if his vocabulary of megalomaniac phrases was limited because he was new to it. But he tossed out a few classics like "I'll show you!" and "You haven't heard the last of me!" before running out of the gym.

Becky started giving orders, and kids started bustling. Magda and I looked at each other. We were both covered in slime and ceiling dust. But we'd done it. We'd saved everybody. And I was kicked off the committee.

"What are we still doing here?" said Magda.

16

WINTER WONDERLAND

As much as my backyard resisted improvement, it also resisted harm. It was Saturday evening, only six hours since we got back from the gym, and all the Slug ooze had been absorbed, as well as all the leaves the Moles had taped on. And the tombstones seemed more covered in bat poop than ever.

Everything had gone back to looking exactly how it was. Which, to Moles, was beautiful. The dead brush and leafless tree limbs that reminded them of roots made the place a garden of Eden in their eyes.

And the perfect place for a young Mole to ask the love of his life to marry him.

Lindoog said yes, she would be his bride, and the two squeezed each other so hard dirt fell out of their crevices.

They thanked me, saying they'd never have found their path to each other if it wasn't for me. I said I was happy to have helped Ploogoo with his poetry and scarf choices, and Lindoog begged me to never help in that way again.

Then I heard my dad whistling his way up the hill toward us. Ploogoo and Lindoog started to jump into the grave hole, but I told them to wait.

I'd been doing everything in my power to make my dad less weird. But my dad was always going to be weird. It wasn't right for me to keep this wonderful piece of weirdness from him any longer. I wanted them to meet.

"Oh. Who are your friends, Sport?" he said when he saw me standing with the Moles. Sheesh. I know he's comfortable with weird, but when you introduce someone to creatures from the underground, you expect at least a gasp or something.

"They're Mole People," I said, "and congratulations are in order."

"Oh my! Congratulations indeed!" said my dad, gasping at the engagement ring Lindoog dangled under his nose. No gasp for Mole People, but a gasp for a round hunk of stone.

"You have a very beautiful garden, Mr. Doug's Dad," said Lindoog.

"I agree," said my dad, "but we'll probably be moving soon. I want to make sure my Doug grows up in a home that makes him happy."

"Don't worry, Dad," I said. "I don't know why I didn't see it before, but this house is perfect. I'm sorry I tried to get my Mole subjects to change it."

"Subjects?" said my dad.

"Your son isn't just our friend," said Ploogoo. "He's also our King."

My dad was elated. "My son . . . a king!" He beamed, hugging me hard.

I told him not to be so proud, because I'd used my crown irresponsibly, getting the Moles to do manual labor and putting them at risk of getting seen by scientists, etc. I apologized to Ploogoo and Lindoog for doing that.

"You never needed the crown for that," said Ploogoo. "We would have helped you as friends."

Now they tell me.

"Not everyone is suited to the task of leadership," said Lindoog to my dad. "Your son is a natural at it."

"It's true," said Ploogoo. "In fact, he's king of the Slug People too!"

My dad squished me again, saying, "Too proud! Too proud!"

I told him to keep his proudness under wraps, as I'd already gotten out of that one.

The minute we got back from the gym the Slugs started in about the Slug crown. For a bunch of creatures who moved so slow, they weren't very patient.

They wouldn't let me quit being the Slug King without being beaten in a Great Slugging. So I let Cream Cheese challenge me, and "crush" me so that she became the new leader. The Slugs have a rule about not being able to challenge any

Slugs under a certain "slime goob" (the Slug unit of age measurement), so Cream Cheese will be in charge for now. Apparently there's already been a few royal edicts involving French music and watermelon-flavored breath spray.

CREAM CHEESE TAKES THE CROWN!

I told my dad I was sorry I'd tried to highjack his eel book interview to interest potential house buyers. The TV spot had aired, and it was all about our weird house with its slime-covered yard, and didn't mention the book once. My dad said it didn't matter, as long as I was happy, that's all he really cared about. That, and making sure I was well-fed. He was just coming out to get an eel so he could whip up a batch of my favorite eel burritos.

I told him I couldn't stay for dinner tonight. I had an important appointment with the human ambassador. He looked me up and down, noticing the tie for the first time. He winked at me. Ploogoo covered one of his eyes with his hand. I think that was the Mole version of winking.

I left the three of them chatting about the wedding. My Dad had some exciting ideas about what they could do with the yard to make it all romantic. Great. My dad was the new wedding planner for the nether realms.

I hopped the picket fence and went to Magda's house and knocked on her window.

"I can't believe I agreed to go to this dance," she said, parting the curtains of black ducklings.

Me neither, since she'd only mentioned about fifty times how she wouldn't be caught dead there. I'd pointed out that we saved the whole school. We might as well go dance in it.

"Don't think of it like going to a dance," I said. "Think of it more like taking a victory lap."

"I guess we earned it, defeating your 'vortex of weirdness,'" she said.

"I admit there's no vortex of weirdness surrounding me," I said. "A dead bird falling out of the sky is probably pretty normal. Maybe it led a full life and died completely fulfilled. My weirdness theory was just an excuse because I was scared."

"But you faced your fears. And now you're free."

Whoa, slow down. I was still pretty scared of a lot of things. But maybe I was a tiny bit more free from fear of weirdness and giant Slugs. No, scratch that, I was more afraid of giant Slugs than ever.

Magda stepped out the window into the dusk. She'd also spruced up for the evening. We felt like a couple of celebrities.

"You know how to tie a tie?" she asked.

"Of course," I said, hoping the clip wasn't showing.

ALL BLACK AS USUAL, BUT MASCARA SHINY INSTEAD OF MATTE

CLIP-ON TIE (STILL HARD TO PUT ON)

We felt even more like celebrities when we arrived at the school to find TV crews waiting. They'd heard a number of rumors—strange beings sighted around the schoolyard, slimy windows, mysterious piles of bricks blocking doorways and then disappearing. When they spotted me—the boy from the house with the slimed backyard— they ran up and started asking me questions. I took the opportunity to tell everyone about my Dad's awesome book of eel recipes.

The dance had been "saved" by Becky. She

turned the theme into "Winter Wonderland" and sprayed everything with white snow to cover all the problems. She even turned the wrecked Eiffel Tower into a ski slope. The fake snow covered what was left of the slime and made it into packing snow, so everyone could have snowball fights. Becky sat cross-legged on an elevated platform while the Binkettes praised her and told her how much they now appreciated how hard it must be to be in charge of things. I snorted. Being in charge of one thing? Amateur.

Marco was the most relieved of all that the dance was saved. He was able to debut his new European scarf. Unfortunately for him he talked about it too loud in front of Ed and Ted. They were pretty upset about the condition of their beloved gym and were happy to find a target to take it out on.

The winter wonderfulness of this sight was undermined by Principal Wiggins. He made a beeline for me and started chewing me out for abandoning the committee, skipping school, almost ruining the dance, not reporting on Miss

Chips like I was supposed to, and probably lots more, I'm not really sure, I stopped listening. Note to adults: if you're chewing out a kid, pick a topic. We zone out even quicker than you think we do.

Principal Wiggins was clearly afraid of Miss Chips. "Stand up to your fears, Principal Wiggins," I told him. "It'll set you free."

He looked at me and then at Miss Chips. I handed him a bag and indicated with my eyes that he should give it to her. He accepted it hopefully and transferred it across the room to Chips.

"What's in the bag?" asked Magda.

"Eel French fries with mayonnaise," I said. "I heard that's the way they eat fries in Paris."

Miss Chips sniffed the bag's contents, and without even looking up at Principal Wiggins, dropped some marshmallows onto the mayonnaise and started eating. I guess that was as close to a declaration of peace as anyone could hope for with Miss Chips.

A slow song came on, and Magda and I realized we were standing in the middle of the gym, so we started dancing. Which just consisted of putting our hands together and rocking back and forth like we were trying to keep our balance on a boat.

"That was some ordeal, huh?" said Magda.

"Yes, definitely an ordeal," I said.

"So did we become 'closer' to each other?" she said.

"I don't know. Do you think so?"

"I don't know. Maybe a bit."

"Yeah. Maybe just a tiny bit."

"Or maybe we were right. Maybe ordeals only work on Moles," she said.

"Yeah, maybe," I said.

We balanced on a boat some more.

"Hey, wait," I said. "When I was on the Eiffel Tower and it was crashing to the ground. Did I hear you call me by my actual first name? Did you call me . . . Doug?"

"Hey, is that a crown?" said Magda, looking over my shoulder.

I looked where she was indicating. There was a crown drawn in the snow/slime slush. How the heck—?

"Hey, guys!" said a snowman who had moved up beside us. We looked into its mouth and saw an even bigger mouth.

"Oog!" I said.

"What are you doing here?" asked Magda.

Oog told us that Pennyworth was seen back in the caves looking for more Slug eggs. Fortunately the Slugs had moved them all out of the egg chamber. Pennyworth was last spotted heading deeper into the earth to look for them, yelling more megalomaniac clichés and slipping and doing splits.

"Maybe he and Croogy will find each other," I said.

Oog also told us that after seeing everyone band together to help them, the Bull Slugs finally felt respected, and had withdrawn their demands for compensation from the Moles.

But! There was a new problem! On the even lower levels! And it really needed my attention—

I cut snowman Oog off.

"Oog, you're a great friend," I said. "I promise I'll appreciate you more, and that we'll always be friends."

"Oog know what King is going to say next," said Oog. "King going to quit being King. And this time it not joke."

"No, it's not that," I said. "It's just that, I'm sort of busy at the moment." I did that wide-eyed, head-tilt thing that you do when you're trying to subtly draw someone's attention to something right under their nose.

"Ooooooooh!" said Oog, beaming happily. "King and Dark Eyes dancing! Oog get it. Oog give some space. Make himself quiet over by ski slope. You not even know Oog here."

We continued dancing, even as snowballs started flying. Oog was engaged in a snowball fight with a number of other kids who would have freaked if they'd known the snowman they were throwing snowballs at was a Mole man who lived deep below the surface of the earth.

Some kids noticed us together and started saying they were going to put us in a weirdness circle. We beat them to it, drawing a circle around ourselves, telling everybody that nobody was allowed in the circle but us.

Then Magda did that knowing smile she always does, like she already knew what was about to happen, like she thinks she knows everything. But she definitely didn't know everything in this case. I could have easily chickened out.

Grrr. I hate it when she's right.

"Well, what do you know," said Magda. "I guess ordeals *do* work on humans."

"I guess they do," I said.

I can't say I was all the way to where Magda

was on the not-caring-what-anybody-thought thing. But I was getting closer. At that moment, in the weirdness circle, I began to feel at home. Maybe this was exactly where I belonged. Maybe being King of the Mole People was indeed an amazing experience that I should just accept and embrace.

After all, who else were they going to get to do it?

NEXT:

QUEEN OF THE MOLE PEOPLE

Paul Gilligan is the creator of *King of the Mole People* as well as the syndicated comic strip *Pooch Café* and has won awards for both illustration and design for such publications as *Entertainment Weekly*, the *Wall Street Journal*, and *MAD* magazine. He lives in Toronto, Canada, with his family.

paulgilligan.com